Thomas H. Huxley

Technical education and other essays

Thomas H. Huxley

Technical education and other essays

ISBN/EAN: 9783742833280

Manufactured in Europe, USA, Canada, Australia, Japa

Cover: Foto ©Andreas Hilbeck / pixelio.de

Manufactured and distributed by brebook publishing software
(www.brebook.com)

Thomas H. Huxley

Technical education and other essays

TECHNICAL EDUCATION,

AND OTHER ESSAYS.

Viz., The Biological Sciences and Medicine; Joseph Priestley; Sensation and the Sensiferous Organs; Certain Errors Attributed to Aristotle.

By THOMAS H. HUXLEY, F.R.S.

I.

TECHNICAL EDUCATION.*

Any candid observer of the phenomena of modern society will readily admit that bores must be classed among the enemies of the human race; and a little consideration will probably lead him to the further admission, that no species of that extensive genus of noxious creatures is more objectionable than the educational bore. Convinced as I am of the truth of this great social generalization, it is not without a certain trepidation that I venture to address you on an educational topic. For, in the course of the last ten years, to go back no farther, I am afraid to say how often I have ventured to speak of education, from that given in the primary schools to that which is to be had in the universities and medical colleges; indeed, the only part of this wide region into which, as yet, I have not adventured is that into which I propose to intrude to-day.

* Address to the Working Men's Club, London.

Thus, I cannot but be aware that I am dangerously near becoming the thing which all men fear and fly. But I have deliberately elected to run the risk. For when you did me the honor to ask me to address you, an unexpected circumstance had led me to occupy myself seriously with the question of technical education; and I had acquired the conviction that there are few subjects respecting which it is more important for all classes of the community to have clear and just ideas than this; while, certainly, there is none which is more deserving of attention by the Working Men's Club and Institute Union.

It is not for me to express an opinion whether the considerations, which I am about to submit to you, will be proved by experience to be just or not; but I will do my best to make them clear. Among the many good things to be found in Lord Bacon's works, none is more full of wisdom than the saying that "truth more easily comes out of error than out of confusion." Clear and consecutive wrong-thinking is the next best thing to right-thinking; so that, if I succeed in clearing your ideas on this topic, I shall have wasted neither your time nor my own.

"Technical education," in the sense in which the term is ordinarily used, and in which I am now employing it, means that sort of education which is specially adapted to the needs of men whose business in life it is to pursue some kind of handicraft; it is, in fact, a fine Greco-Latin equivalent for what in good vernacular English would be called "the teaching of handicrafts." And probably, at this stage of our progress, it may occur to many of you to think of the story of the cobbler and his last, and to say to yourselves, though you will be too polite to put the question openly to me, What does the speaker know practically about this matter? What is his handicraft? I think the question is a very proper one, and unless I were prepared to answer it, I hope satisfactorily, I should have chosen some other theme.

The fact is, I am, and have been, any time these thirty years, a man who works with his hands—a handicraftsman. I do not say this in the broadly metaphorical sense in which fine gentlemen, with all the delicacy of Agag about them, trip to the hustings about election time, and protest that they too are working men. I really mean my words to be taken in their direct, literal, and straightforward sense. In fact, if the most nimble-fingered watchmaker among you will come to my workshop, he may set me to put a watch together, and I will set him to dissect, say, a blackbeetle's nerves. I do not wish to vaunt, but I am inclined to think that I shall manage my job to his satisfaction sooner than he will do his piece of work to mine.

In truth, anatomy, which is my handicraft, is one of the most difficult kinds of mechanical labor, involving, as it does, not only lightness and dexterity of hand, but sharp eyes and endless patience. And you must not suppose that my particular branch of science is especially distinguished for the demand it makes upon skill in manipulation. A similar requirement is made upon all students of physical science. The astronomer, the electrician, the chemist, the mineralogist, the botanist, are constantly called upon to perform manual operations of exceeding delicacy. The progress of all branches of physical science depends upon observation, or on that artificial observation which is termed experiment, of one kind or another; and, the farther we advance, the more practical difficulties surround the investigation of the conditions of the problems offered to us; so that mobile and yet steady hands, guided by clear vision, are more and more in request in the workshops of science.

Indeed, it has struck me that one of the grounds of that sympathy between the handicraftsmen of this country and the men of science, by which it has so often been my good fortune to profit, may, perhaps, lie here. You feel and we feel that, among the so-called learned folks, we alone are brought into contact with tangible facts in the way that you are. You know well enough that it is one thing to write a history of chairs in general, or to address a poem to a throne, or to speculate about the occult powers of the chair of St. Peter; and quite another thing to make with your own hands a veritable chair, that will stand fair and square, and afford a safe and satisfactory resting-place to a frame of sensitiveness and solidity.

So it is with us, when we look out from our scientific handicrafts upon the doings of our learned brethren, whose work is untrammeled by anything "base and mechanical," as handicrafts used to be called when the world was younger, and in some respects less wise than now. We take the greatest interest in their pursuits; We are edified by their histories and are charmed with their poems, which sometimes illustrate so remarkably the powers of man's imagination; some of us admire and even humbly try to follow them in their high philosophical excursions, though we know the risk of being snubbed by the inquiry whether groveling dissectors of monkeys and blackbeetles can hope to enter into the empyreal kingdom of speculation. But still we feel that our business is different; humbler if you will, though the diminution of dignity is, perhaps, compensated by the increase of reality; and that we, like you, have to get our work done in a region where little avails, if the power of dealing with practical tangible facts is wanting. You know that clever talk touching joinery will not make a chair; and I know that it is of about as much value in the physical sciences. Mother Nature is serenely obdurate to honeyed words; only those who understand the ways of things, and can silently and effectually handle them, get any good out of her.

And now, having, as I hope, justified my assumption of a place among handicraftsmen, and put myself right with you as to my qualification, from practical knowledge, to speak about technical education, I will proceed to lay before you the results of my experience as a teacher of a handicraft, and tell you what sort of education I should think best adapted for a boy whom one wanted to make a professional anatomist.

I should say, in the first place, let him have a good English elementary education. I do not mean that he shall be able to pass in such and such a standard—that may or may not be an equivalent expression—but that his teaching shall have been such as to have given him command of the common implements of learning and to have created a desire for the things of the understanding.

Further, I should like him to know the elements of physical science, and especially of physics and chemistry, and I should take care that this elementary knowledge was real. I should like my aspirant to be able to read a scientific treatise in Latin, French, or German, because an enormous amount of anatomical knowledge is locked up in those languages.

And especially, I should require some ability to draw—I do not mean artistically, for that is a gift which may be cultivated but cannot be learned, but with fair accuracy. I will not say that everybody can learn even this; for the negative development of the faculty of drawing in some people is almost miraculous. Still everybody, or almost everybody, can learn to write; and, as writing is a kind of drawing, I suppose that the majority of the people who say they cannot draw, and give copious evidence of the accuracy of their assertion, could draw, after a fashion, if they tried. And that " after a fashion " would be better than nothing for my purposes.

Above all things, let my imaginary pupil have preserved the freshness and vigor of youth in his mind as well as his body. The educational abomination of desolation of the present day is the stimulation of young people to work at high pressure by incessant competitive examinations. Some wise man (who probably was not an early riser) has said of early risers in general, that they are conceited all the forenoon and stupid all the afternoon. Now whether this is true of early risers in the common acceptation of the word or not, I will not pretend to say; but it is too often true of the unhappy children who are forced to rise too early in their classes. They are conceited all the forenoon of life, and stupid all its afternoon. The vigor and freshness, which should have been stored up for the purposes of the hard struggle for existence in practical life, have been washed out of them by precocious mental debauchery—by book gluttony and lesson bibbing. Their faculties are worn out by the strain put upon their callow brains, and they are demoralized by worthless childish triumphs before the real work of life begins. I have no compassion for sloth, but youth has more need for intellectual rest than age; and the cheerfulness, the tenacity of purpose, the power of work which make many a successful man what he is, must often be placed

to the credit, not of his hours of industry, but to that of his hours of idle-
ness, in boyhood. Even the hardest
worker of us all, if he has to deal with
anything above mere details, will do
well, now and again, to let his brain
lie fallow for a space. The next crop
of thought will certainly be all the
fuller in the ear and the weeds fewer.

This is the sort of education which
I should like any one who was going
to devote himself to my handicraft to
undergo. As to knowing anything
about anatomy itself, on the whole I
would rather he left that alone until
he took it up seriously in my laboratory. It is hard work enough to teach,
and I should not like to have superadded to that the possible need of
unteaching.

Well, but, you will say, this is
Hamlet with the Prince of Denmark
left out; your "technical education"
is simply a good education, with more
attention to physical science, to drawing, and to modern languages, than is
common, and there is nothing specially technical about it.

Exactly so; that remark takes us
straight to the heart of what I have to
say; which is, that, in my judgment,
the preparatory education of the
handicraftsman ought to have nothing of what is ordinarily understood
by " technical " about it.

The workshop is the only real
school for a handicraft. The education which precedes that of the workshop should be entirely devoted to
the strengthening of the body, the
elevation of the moral faculties, and
the cultivation of the intelligence;
and, especially, to the imbuing the
mind with a broad and clear view of
the laws of that natural world with
the components of which the handicraftsman will have to deal. And,
the earlier the period of life at which
the handicraftsman has to enter into
actual practice of his craft, the more
important is it that he should devote
the precious hours of preliminary education to things of the mind, which
have no direct and immediate bearing
on his branch of industry, though

they lie at the foundation of all realities.

Now let me apply the lessons I
have learned from my handicraft to
yours. If any of you were obliged to
take an apprentice, I suppose you
would like to get a good healthy lad,
ready and willing to learn, handy, and
with his fingers not all thumbs, as the
saying goes. You would like that he
should read, write, and cipher well;
and, if you were an intelligent master,
and your trade involved the application of scientific principles, as so
many trades do, you would like him
to know enough of the elementary
principles of science to understand
what was going on. I suppose that,
in nine trades out of ten, it would be
useful if he could draw; and many
of you must have lamented your inability to find out for yourselves what
foreigners are doing or have done.
So that some knowledge of French
and German might, in many cases, be
very desirable.

So it appears to me that what you
want is pretty much what I want;
and the practical question is, How
you are to get what you need, under
the actual limitations and conditions
of life of handicraftsmen in this country.

I think I shall have the assent both
of the employers of labor and of the
employed as to one of these limitations; which is, that no scheme of
technical education is likely to be seriously entertained which will delay
the entrance of boys into working life,
or prevent them from contributing toward their own support, as early as
they do at present. Not only do I believe that any such scheme could not
be carried out, but I doubt its desira-
bleness, even if it were practicable.

The period between childhood and
manhood is full of difficulties and
dangers, under the most favorable circumstances; and, even among the
well-to-do, who can afford to surround
their children with the most favorable
conditions, examples of a career
ruined, before it has well begun, are
but too frequent. Moreover, those

who have to live by labor must be shaped to labor early. The colt that is left at grass too long makes but a sorry draught-horse, though his way of life does not bring him within the reach of artificial temptations. Perhaps the most valuable result of all education is the ability to make yourself do the thing you have to do, when it ought to be done, whether you like it or not; it is the first lesson that ought to be learned; and, however early a man's training begins, it is probably the last lesson that he learns thoroughly.

There is another reason, to which I have already adverted, and which I would reiterate, why any extension of the time devoted to ordinary school-work is undesirable. In the newly awakened zeal for education, we run some risk of forgetting the truth that while under-instruction is a bad thing, over-instruction may possibly be a worse.

Success in any kind of practical life is not dependent solely, or indeed chiefly, upon knowledge. Even in the learned professions, knowledge, alone, is of less consequence than people are apt to suppose. And, if much expenditure of bodily energy is involved in the day's work, mere knowledge is of still less importance when weighed against the probable cost of its acquirement. To do a fair day's work with his hands, a man needs, above all things, health, strength, and the patience and cheerfulness which, if they do not always accompany these blessings, can hardly in the nature of things exist without them; to which we must add honesty of purpose and a pride in doing what is done well.

A good handicraftsman can get on very well without genius, but he will fare badly without a reasonable share of that which is a more useful possession for workaday life, namely, mother-wit; and he will be all the better for a real knowledge, however limited, of the ordinary laws of nature, and especially of those which apply to his own business.

Instruction carried so far as to help the scholar to turn his store of mother-wit to account, to acquire a fair amount of sound elementary knowledge, and to use his hands and eyes; while leaving him fresh, vigorous, and with a sense of the dignity of his own calling, whatever it may be, if fairly and honestly pursued, cannot fail to be of invaluable service to all those who come under its influence.

But, on the other hand, if school instruction is carried so far as to encourage bookishness; if the ambition of the scholar is directed, not to the gaining of knowledge, but to the being able to pass examinations successfully; especially if encouragement is given to the mischievous delusion that brainwork is, in itself, and apart from its quality, a nobler or more respectable thing than handiwork—such education may be a deadly mischief to the workman, and lead to the rapid ruin of the industries it is intended to serve.

I know that I am expressing the opinion of some of the largest as well as the most enlightened employers of labor, when I say that there is a real danger that, from the extreme of no education, we may run to the other extreme of over-education of handicraftsmen. And I apprehend that what is true for the ordinary hand-worker is true for the foreman. Activity, probity, knowledge of men, ready mother-wit, supplemented by a good knowledge of the general principles involved in his business, are the making of a good foreman. If he possess these qualities, no amount of learning will fit him better for his position; while the course of life and the habit of mind required for the attainment of such learning may, in various direct and indirect ways, act as direct disqualifications for it.

Keeping in mind, then, that the two things to be avoided are, the delay of the entrance of boys into practical life, and the substitution of exhausted bookworms for shrewd, handy men, in our works and factories, let us consider what may be wisely and safely attempted in the way of improving the education of the handicraftsman.

First, I look to the elementary schools now happily established all over the country. I am not going to criticise or find fault with them; on the contrary, their establishment seems to me to be the most important and the most beneficial result of the corporate action of the people in our day. A great deal is said of British interests just now, but, depend upon it, that no Eastern difficulty needs our intervention as a nation so seriously, as the putting down both the Bashi-Bazouks of ignorance and the Cossacks of sactarianism at home. What has already been achieved in these directions is a great thing; you must have lived some time to know how great. An education, better in its processes, better in its substance, than that which was accessible to the great majority of well-to-do Britons a quarter of a century ago, is now obtainable by every child in the land. Let any man of my age go into an ordinary elementary school, and, unless he was unusually fortunate in his youth, he will tell you that the educational method, the intelligence, patience, and good temper on the teacher's part, which are now at the disposal of the veriest waifs and wastrels of society, are things of which he had no experience in those costly middle-class schools, which were so ingeniously contrived as to combine all the evils and shortcomings of the great public schools with none of their advantages. Many a man, whose so-called education cost a good deal of valuable money and occupied many a year of invaluable time, leaves the inspection of a well-ordered elementary school devoutly wishing that, in his young days, he had had the chance of being as well taught as these boys and girls are.

But while in view of such an advance in general education, I willingly obey the natural impulse to be thankful, I am not willing altogether to rest. I want to see instruction in elementary science and in art more thoroughly incorporated in the educational system. At present, it is being administered by driblets, as if it were a potent medicine, "a few drops to be taken occasionally in a teaspoon." Every year I notice that that earnest and untiring friend of yours and of mine, Sir John Lubbock, stirs up the Government of the day in the House of Commons on this subject; and also that, every year, he and the few members of the House of Commons, such as Mr. Playfair, who sympathize with him, are met with expressions of warm admiration for science in general, and reasons at large for doing nothing in particular. But now that Mr. Forster, to whom the education of the country owes so much, has announced his conversion to the right faith, I begin to hope that, sooner or later, things will mend.

I have given what I believe to be a good reason for the assumption; that the keeping at school of boys who are to be handicraftsmen, beyond the age of thirteen or fourteen is neither practicable nor desirable; and, as it is quite certain, that with justice to other and no less important branches of education, nothing more than the rudiments of science and art teaching can be introduced into elementary schools, we must seek elsewhere for a supplementary training in these subjects, and, if need be, in foreign languages, which may go on after the workman's life has begun.

The means of acquiring the scientific and artistic part of this training already exists in full working order, in the first place, in the classes of the Science and Art Department, which are, for the most part, held in the evening, so as to be accessible to all who choose to avail themselves of them after working hours. The great advantage of these classes is that they bring the means of instruction to the doors of the factories and workshops; that they are no artificial creations, but by their very existence prove the desire of the people for them; and finally, that they admit of indefinite development in proportion as they are wanted. I have often expressed the opinion, and I repeat it here, that, during the eighteen years they have been in existence, these classes have done incalculable good; and I can say, of my own knowledge, that the Department spares no pains and trouble in trying to increase their usefulness and ensure the soundness of their work.

No one knows better than my friend Colonel Donnelly, to whose clear views and great administrative abilities so much of the successful working of the science classes is due, that there is much to be done before the system can be said to be thoroughly satisfactory. The instruction given needs to be made more systematic and especially more practical; the teachers are of very unequal excellence, and not a few stand much in need of instruction themselves, not only in the subjects which they teach, but in the objects for which they teach. I daresay you have heard of that proceeding, reprobated by all true sportsmen, which is called " shooting for the pot." Well, there is such a thing as " teaching for the pot "—teaching, that is, not that your scholar may know, but that he may count for payment among those who pass the examination ; and there are some teachers, happily not many, who have yet to learn that the examiners of the Department regard them as poachers of the worst description.

Without presuming in any way to speak in the name of the Department, I think I may say, as a matter which has come under my own observation, that it is doing its best to meet all these difficulties. It systematically promotes practical instruction in the classes; it affords facilities to teachers who desire to learn their business thoroughly ; and it is always ready to aid in the suppression of pot-teaching.

All this is, as you may imagine, highly satisfactory to me. I see that spread of scientific education, about which I have so often permitted myself to worry the public, become, for all practical purposes, an accomplished fact. Grateful as I am for all

that is now being done, in the same direction, in our higher schools and universities, I have ceased to have any anxiety about the wealthier classes. Scientific knowledge is spreading by what the alchemists called a "distillatio per ascensum ;" and nothing now can prevent it from continuing to distil upward and permeate English society until, in the remote future, there shall be no member of the legislature who does not know as much of science as an elementary school-boy; and even the heads of houses in our venerable seats of learning shall acknowledge that natural science is not merely a sort of University backdoor through which inferior men may get at their degrees. Perhaps this apocalyptic vision is a little wild; and I feel I ought to ask pardon for an outbreak of enthusiasm, which, I assure you, is not my commonest failing.

I have said that the Government is already doing a great deal in aid of that kind of technical education for handicraftsmen which, to my mind, is alone worth seeking. Perhaps it is doing as much as it ought to do, even in this direction. Certainly there is another kind of help of the most important character, for which we may look elsewhere than to the Government. The great mass of mankind have neither the liking, or the aptitude, for either literary, or scientific, or artistic pursuits ; nor, indeed, for excellence of any sort. Their ambition is to go through life with moderate exertion and a fair share of ease, doing common things in a common way. And a great blessing and comfort it is that the majority of men are of this mind ; for the majority of things to be done are common things, and are quite well enough done when commonly done. The great end of life is not knowledge but action. What men need is, as much knowledge as they can assimilate and organize into a basis for action ; give them more and it may become injurious. One knows people who are as heavy and stupid from undigested learning as others are from overfulness of meat and drink. But a small percentage of the population is born with that most excellent quality, a desire for excellence, or with special aptitudes of some sort or another; Mr. Galton tells us that not more than one in four thousand may be expected to attain distinction, and not more than one in a million, some share of that intensity of instinctive aptitude, that burning thirst for excellence, which is called genius.

Now, the most important object of all educational schemes is to catch these exceptional people, and turn them to account for the good of society. No man can say where they will crop up; like their opposites, the fools and knaves, they appear sometimes in the palace, and sometimes in the hovel; but the great thing to be aimed at, I was almost going to say the most important end of all social arrangements, is to keep these glorious sports of Nature from being either corrupted by luxury or starved by poverty, and to put them into the position in which they can do the work for which they are specially fitted.

Thus, if a lad in an elementary school showed signs of special capacity, I would try to provide him with the means of continuing his education after his daily working life had begun; if, in the evening classes, he developed special capabilities in the direction of science or of drawing, I would try to secure him an apprenticeship to some trade in which those powers would have applicability. Or, if he chose to become a teacher, he should have the chance of so doing. Finally, to the lad of genius, the one in a million, I would make accessible the highest and most complete training the country could afford. Whatever that might cost depend upon it the investment would be a good one. I weigh my words when I say that if the nation could purchase a potential Watt, or Davy, or Faraday, at the cost of a hundred thousand pounds down, he would be dirt-cheap at the money. It is a mere commonplace and everyday piece of knowledge, that what these three men did has produced untold millions of wealth, in the narrowest economical sense of the word.

Therefore, as the sum and crown of what is to be done for technical education, I look to the provision of a machinery for winnowing out the capacities and giving them scope. When I was a member of the London School Board, I said, in the course of a speech, that our business was to provide a ladder, reaching from the gutter to the university, along which every child in the three kingdoms should have the chance of climbing as far as he was fit to go. This phrase was so much bandied about at the time, that, to say the truth, I am rather tired of it, but I know of no other which so fully expresses my belief, not only about education in general, but about technical education in particular.

The essential foundation of all the organization needed for the promotion of education among handicraftsmen will, I believe, exist in this country, when every working lad can feel that society has done as much as lies in its power to remove all needless and artificial obstacles from his path; that there is no barrier, except such as exists in the nature of things, between himself and whatever place in the social organization he is fitted to fill; and, more than this, that, if he has capacity and industry, a hand is held out to help him along any path which is wisely and honestly chosen.

I have endeavored to point out to you that a great deal of such an organization already exists; and I am glad to be able to add that there is a good prospect that what is wanted will, before long, be supplemented.

Those powerful and wealthy societies, the livery companies of the City of London, remembering that they are the heirs and representatives of the trade guilds of the Middle Ages, are interesting themselves in the question. So far back as 1872 the Society of Arts organized a system of instruction in the technology of arts and manufactures, for persons actually employed in factories and workshops, who desired to extend and improve their knowledge of the theory and practice of their particular avocations ; * and a considerable subsidy, in aid of the efforts of the Society, was liberally granted by the Clothworkers' Company. We have here the hopeful commencement of a rational organization for the promotion of excellence among handicraftsmen. Quite recently, other of the livery companies have determined upon giving their powerful, and, indeed, almost boundless, aid to the improvement of the teaching of handicrafts. They have already gone so far as to appoint a committee to act for them ; and I betray no confidence in adding that, some time since, the committee sought the advice and assistance of several persons, myself among the number.

Of course I cannot tell you what may be the result of the deliberations of the committe ; but we may all fairly hope that, before long, steps which will have a weighty and a lasting influence on the growth and spread of sound and thorough teaching among the handicraftsmen † of this country will be taken by the livery companies of London.

[This hope has been fully justified by the establishment of the Cowper Street Schools, and that of the Central Institution of the City and Guilds of London Institute.]

II.

THE CONNECTION OF THE BIOLOGICAL SCIENCES WITH MEDICINE.‡

THE great body of theoretical and practical knowledge which has been accumulated by the labors of some eighty generations, since the dawn of scientific thought in Europe, has no collective English name to which an objection may not be raised ; and 1 use the term "medicine" as that which is least likely to be misunderstood ; though, as every one knows, the name is commonly applied, in a narrower sense, to one of the chief divisions of the totality of medical science.

Taken in this broad sense, "medicine" not merely denotes a kind of knowledge, but it comprehends the various applications of that knowledge to the alleviation of the sufferings, the repair of the injuries, and the conservation of the health, of living beings. In fact, the practical aspect of medicine so far dominates over every other, that the "Healing Art" is one of its most widely-received synonyms. It is so difficult to think of medicine otherwise than as something which is necessarily connected with curative treatment, that we are apt to forget that there must be, and is, such a thing as a pure science of medicine— a "pathology" which has no more necessary subservience to practical ends than has zoology or botany.

The logical connection between this purely scientific doctrine of disease, or pathology, and ordinary biology, is easily traced. Living matter is characterized by its innate tendency to exhibit a definite series of the morphological and physiological phenomena which constitute organization and life. Given a certain range of conditions, and these phenomena remain the same, within narrow limits, for each kind of living thing. They furnish the normal and typical character of the species, and as such, they are the subject-matter of ordinary biology.

Outside the range of these conditions, the normal course of the cycle of vital phenomena is disturbed ; abnormal structure makes its appearance, or the proper character and mutual adjustment of the functions cease to be preserved. The extent and the importance of these deviations

---

* See the "Programme" for 1878, issued by the Society of Arts, p. 14.
† It is perhaps advisable to remark that the important question of the professional education of managers of industrial works is not touched in the foregoing remarks.
‡ Address at the International Medical College, London, 1881.

from the typical life may vary indefi-
nitely. They may have no noticeable
influence on the general well-being of
the economy, or they may favor it.
On the other hand, they may be of
such a nature as to impede the activities of the organism, or even to in-
volve its destruction.

In the first case, these perturbations are ranged under the wide and
somewhat vague category of "variations;" in the second, they are called
lesions, states of poisoning, or diseases; and, as morbid states, they
lie within the province of pathology.
No sharp line of demarkation can be
drawn between the two classes of phenomena. No one can say where anatomical variations end and tumors
begin, nor where modification of function, which may at first promote
health, passes into disease. All that
can be said is, that whatever change
of structure or function is hurtful be-
longs to pathology. Hence it is obvious that pathology is a branch of biology; it is the morphology, the physiology, the distribution, the ætiology
of abnormal life.

However obvious this conclusion
may be now, it was nowise apparent
in the infancy of medicine. For it is
a peculiarity of the physical sciences,
that they are independent in proportion as they are imperfect; and it is
only as they advance that the bonds
which really unite them all become
apparent. Astronomy had no manifest connection with terrestrial physics before the publication of the
"Principia;" that of chemistry with
physics is of still more modern revelation; that of physics and chemistry
with physiology, has been stoutly denied within the recollection of most
of us, and perhaps still may be.

Or, to take a case which affords a
closer parallel with that of medicine.
Agriculture has been cultivated from
the earliest times, and, from a remote
antiquity, men have attained considerable practical skill in the cultivation
of the useful plants, and have empiric-
ally established many scientific truths
concerning the conditions under which

they flourish. But, it is within the
memory of many of us, that chemistry
on the one hand, and vegetable physiology on the other, attained a stage
of development such that they were
able to furnish a sound basis for scientific agriculture. Similarly, medicine took its rise in the practical
needs of mankind. At first, studied
without reference to any other branch
of knowledge, it long maintained, indeed still to some extent maintains,
that independence. Historically, its
connection with the biological sciences has been slowly established, and
the full extent and intimacy of that
connection are only now beginning to
be apparent. I trust I have not been
mistaken in supposing that an attempt
to give a brief sketch of the steps by
which a philosophical necessity has
become an historical reality, may not
be devoid of interest, possibly of instruction, to the members of this
great Congress, profoundly interested
as all are in the scientific development of medicine.

The history of medicine is more
complete and fuller than that of any
other science, except, perhaps, astronomy; and, if we follow back the long
record as far as clear evidence lights
us, we find ourselves taken to the
early stages of the civilization of
Greece. The oldest hospitals were
the temples of Æsculapius; to these
Asclepeia, always erected on healthy
sites, hard by fresh springs and surrounded by shady groves, the sick
and the maimed resorted to seek the
aid of the god of health. Votive tab-
lets or inscriptions recorded the symptoms, no less than the gratitude, of
those who were healed; and, from
these primitive clinical records, the
half-priestly, half-philosophic caste of
the Asclepiads compiled the data
upon which the earliest generalizations of medicine, as an inductive
science, were based.

In this state, pathology, like all the
inductive sciences at their origin, was
merely natural history; it registered
the phenomena of disease, classified
them, and ventured upon a prognosis,

wherever the observation of constant co-existences and sequences suggested a rational expectation of the like recurrence under similar circumstances.

Further than this it hardly went. In fact, in the then state of knowledge, and in the condition of philosophical speculation at that time, neither the causes of the morbid state, nor the *rationale* of treatment, were likely to be sought for as we seek for them now. The anger of a god was a sufficient reason for the existence of a malady, and a dream ample warranty for therapeutic measures; that a physical phenomenon must needs have a physical cause was not the implied or expressed axiom that it is to us moderns.

The great man whose name is inseparably connected with the foundation of medicine, Hippocrates, certainly knew very little, indeed practically nothing, of anatomy or physiology; and he would, probably, have been perplexed, even to imagine the possibility of a connection between the zoological studies of his contemporary Democritus and medicine. Nevertheless, in so far as he, and those who worked before and after him, in the same spirit, ascertained, as matters of experience, that a wound, or a luxation, or a fever, presented such and such symptoms, and that the return of the patient to health was facilitated by such and such measures, they established laws of nature, and began the construction of the science of pathology. All true science begins with empiricism— though all true science is such exactly, in so far as it strives to pass out of the empirical stage into that of the deduction of empirical from more general truths. Thus, it is not wonderful, that the early physicians had little or nothing to do with the development of biological science; and, on the other hand, that the early biologists did not much concern themselves with medicine. There is nothing to show that the Asclepiads took any prominent share in the work of founding anatomy, physiology, zoology, and botany. Rather do these seem to have sprung from the early philosophers, who were essentially natural philosophers, animated by the characteristically Greek thirst for knowledge as such. Pythagoras, Alcmeon, Democritus, Diogenes of Apollonia, are all credited with anatomical and physiological investigations; and though Aristotle is said to have belonged to an Asclepiad family, and not improbably owed his taste for anatomical and zoological inquiries to the teachings of his father, the physician Nicomachus, the "Historia Animalium," and the treatise "De Partibus Animalium," are as free from any allusion to medicine as if they had issued from a modern biological laboratory.

It may be added, that it is not easy to see in what way it could have benefited a physician of Alexander's time to know all that Aristotle knew on these subjects. His human anatomy was too rough to avail much in diagnosis; his physiology was too erroneous to supply data for pathological reasoning. But when the Alexandrian school, with Erasistratus and Herophilus at their head, turned to account the opportunities of studying human structure, afforded to them by the Ptolemies, the value of the large amount of accurate knowledge thus obtained to the surgeon for his operations, and to the physician for his diagnosis of internal disorders, became obvious, and a connection was established between anatomy and medicine, which has ever become closer and closer. Since the revival of learning, surgery, medical diagnosis, and anatomy have gone hand in hand. Morgagni called his great work, "De sedibus et causis morborum per anatomen indagatis," and not only showed the way to search out the localities and the causes of disease by anatomy, but himself traveled wonderfully far upon the road. Bichat, discriminating the grosser constituents of the organs and parts of the body, one from another, pointed out the direction which modern research must take ; until, at length, histology, a science of yesterday, as it seems to many of us, has carried the work of Morgagni as far as the microscope can take us, and has extended the realm of pathological anatomy to the limits of the invisible world.

Thanks to the intimate alliance of morphology with medicine, the natural history of disease has, at the present day, attained a high degree of perfection. Accurate regional anatomy has rendered practicable the exploration of the most hidden parts of the organism, and the determination, during life, of morbid changes in them ; anatomical and histological post-mortem investigations have supplied physicians with a clear basis upon which to rest the classification of diseases, and with unerring tests of the accuracy or inaccuracy of their diagnoses.

If men could be satisfied with pure knowledge, the extreme precision with which, in these days, a sufferer may be told what is happening, and what is likely to happen, even in the most recondite parts of his bodily frame, should be as satisfactory to the patient as it is to the scientific pathologist who gives him the information. But I am afraid it is not; and even the practicing physician, while nowise underestimating the regulative value of accurate diagnosis, must often lament that so much of his knowledge rather prevents him from doing wrong than helps him to do right.

A scorner of physic once said that nature and disease may be compared to two men fighting, the doctor to a blind man with a club, who strikes into the *melée*, sometimes hitting the disease, and sometimes hitting nature. The matter is not mended if you suppose the blind man's hearing to be so acute that he can register every stage of the struggle, and pretty clearly predict how it will end. He had better not meddle at all, until his eyes are opened—until he can see the exact position of the antagonists,

and make sure of the effect of his blows. But that which it behoves the physician to see, not, indeed, with his bodily eye, but with clear, intellectual vision, is a process, and the chain of causation involved in that process. Disease, as we have seen, is a perturbation of the normal activities of a living body, and it is, and must remain, unintelligible, so long as we are ignorant of the nature of these normal activities. In other words, there could be no real science of pathology until the science of physiology had reached a degree of perfection unattained, and indeed unattainable, until quite recent times.

So far as medicine is concerned, I am not sure that physiology, such as it was down to the time of Harvey, might as well not have existed. Nay, it is perhaps no exaggeration to say that, within the memory of living men, justly renowned practitioners of medicine and surgery knew less physiology than is now to be learned from the most elementary text-book ; and, beyond a few broad facts, regarded what they did know as of extremely little practical importance. Nor am I disposed to blame them for this conclusion ; physiology must be useless, or worse than useless, to pathology, so long as its fundamental conceptions are erroneous.

Harvey is often said to be the founder of modern physiology ; and there can be no question that the elucidations of the function of the heart, of the nature of the pulse, and of the course of the blood, put forth in the ever-memorable little essay, "De motu cordis," directly worked a revolution in men's views of the nature and of the concatenation of some of the most important physiological processes among the higher animals; while, indirectly, their influence was perhaps even more remarkable.

But, though Harvey made this signal and perennially important contribution to the physiology of the moderns, his general conception of vital processes was essentially indentical with that of the ancients ; and, in the "Exercitationes de generatione," and notably in the singular chapter "De calido innato," he shows himself a true son of Galen and of Aristotle.

For Harvey, the blood possesses powers superior to those of the elements ; it is the seat of a soul which is not only vegetative, but also sensitive and motor. The blood maintains and fashions all parts of the body, "idque summâ cum providentiâ et intellectu in finem certum agens, quasi ratiocinio quodam uteretur."

Here is the doctrine of the "pneuma," the product of the philosophical mould into which the animism of primitive men ran in Greece, in full force. Nor did its strength abate for long after Harvey's time. The same ingrained tendency of the human mind to suppose that a process is explained when it is ascribed to a power of which nothing is known except that it is the hypothetical agent of the process, gave rise, in the next century, to the animism of Stahl; and, later, to the doctrine of a vital principle, that "asylum ignorantiæ" of physiologists, which has so easily accounted for everything and explained nothing, down to our own times.

Now the essence of modern, as contrasted with ancient, physiological science appears to me to lie in its antagonism to animistic hypotheses and animistic phraseology. It offers physical explanations of vital phenomena, or frankly confesses that it has none to offer. And, so far as I know, the first person who gave expression to this modern view of physiology, who was bold enough to enunciate the proposition that vital phenomena, like all the other phenomena of the physical world, are, in ultimate analysis, resolvable into matter and motion, was René Descartes.

The fifty-four years of life of this most original and powerful thinker are widely overlapped, on both sides, by the eighty of Harvey, who survived his younger contemporary by seven years, and takes pleasure in acknowledging the French philosopher's appreciation of his great discovery.

In fact, Descartes accepted the doctrine of the circulation as propounded by "Harvæus médecin d'Angleterre," and gave a full account of it in his first work, the famous "Discours de la Méthode," which was published in 1637, only nine years after the exercitation "De motu cordis ;" and, though differing from Harvey on some important points (in which it may be noted, in passing, Descartes was wrong and Harvey right), he always speaks of him with great respect. And so important does the subject seem to Descartes, that he returns to it in the "Traité des Passions," and in the "Traité de l'Homme."

It is easy to see that Harvey's work must have had a peculiar significance for the subtle thinker, to whom we owe both the spiritualistic and the materialistic philosophies of modern times. It was in the very year of its publication, 1628, that Descartes withdrew into that life of solitary investigation and meditation of which his philosophy was the fruit. And, as the course of his speculations led him to establish an absolute distinction of nature between the material and the mental worlds, he was logically compelled to seek for the explanation of the phenomena of the material world within itself; and having allotted the realm of thought to the soul, to see nothing but extension and motion in the rest of nature. Descartes uses "thought" as the equivalent of our modern term "consciousness." Thought is the function of the soul, and its only function. Our natural heat and all the movements of the body, says he, do not depend on the soul. Death does not take place from any fault of the soul, but only because some of the principal parts of the body become corrupted. The body of a living man differs from that of a dead man in the same way as a watch or other automaton (that is to say, a machine which moves of itself) when it is wound up and has, in itself, the physical principle of the movements which the mechanism is adapted to perform, differs from the same watch, or other machine, when it is broken, and the physical principle of its movement no longer exists. All the actions which are common to us and the lower animals depend only on the conformation of our organs, and the course which the animal spirits take in the brain, the nerves, and the muscles; in the same way as the movement of a watch is produced by nothing but the force of its spring and the figure of its wheels and other parts.

Descartes' "Treatise on Man" is a sketch of human physiology, in which a bold attempt is made to explain all the phenomena of life, except those of consciousness, by physical reasonings.

To a mind turned in this direction, Harvey's exposition of the heart and vessels as a hydraulic mechanism must have been supremely welcome.

Descartes was not a mere philosophical theorist, but a hard-working dissector and experimenter, and he held the strongest opinion respecting the practical value of the new conception which he was introducing. He speaks of the importance of preserving health, and of the dependence of the mind on the body being so close that, perhaps, the only way of making men wiser and better than they are, is to be sought in medical science. "It is true," says he, "that as medicine is now practiced, it contains little that is very useful; but without any desire to depreciate, I am sure that there is no one, even among professional men, who will not declare that all we know is very little as compared with that which remains to be known; and that we might escape an infinity of diseases of the mind, no less than of the body, and even perhaps from the weakness of old age, if we had sufficient knowledge of their causes, and of all the remedies with which nature has provided us." ("Discours de la Méthode," 6ᵉ partie, Ed. Cousin, p. 193.) So strongly impressed was Descartes with this, that he resolved to spend the rest of his life in trying to acquire such a knowledge of nature as would lead to the construction of a better medical doctrine. (*Ibid.* 6ᵉ partie, Ed. Cousin, pp. 193 and 211.) The anti-Cartesians found material for cheap ridicule in these aspirations of the philosopher; and it is almost needless to say that, in the thirteen years which elapsed between the publication of the "Discours" and the death of Descartes, he did not contribute much to their realization. But, for the next century, all progress in physiology took place along the lines which Descartes laid down.

The greatest physiological and pathological work of the seventeenth century, Borelli's treatise "De Motu Animalium," is, to all intents and purposes, a development of Descartes' fundamental conception; and the same may be said of the physiology and pathology of Boerhaave, whose authority dominated in the medical world of the first half of the eighteenth century.

With the origin of modern chemistry, and of electrical science, in the latter half of the eighteenth century, aids in the analysis of the phenomena of life, of which Descartes could not have dreamed, were offered to the physiologist. And the greater part of the gigantic progress which has been made in the present century is a justification of the prevision of Descartes. For it consists, essentially, in a more and more complete resolution of the grosser organs of the living body into physico-chemical mechanisms.

"I shall try to explain our whole bodily machinery in such a way, that it will be no more necessary for us to suppose that the soul produces such movements as are not voluntary, than it is to think that there is in a clock a soul which causes it to show the hours." ("De la Formation du Fœtus.") These words of Descartes might be appropriately taken as a motto by the author of any modern treatise on physiology.

But though, as I think, there is no

doubt that Descartes was the first to propound the fundamental conception of the living body as a physical mechanism, which is the distinctive feature of modern, as contrasted with ancient physiology, he was misled by the natural temptation to carry out, in all its details, a parallel between the machines with which he was familiar, such as clocks and pieces of hydraulic apparatus, and the living machine. In all such machines there is a central source of power, and the parts of the machine are merely passive distributors of that power. The Cartesian school conceived of the living body as a machine of this kind ; and herein they might have learned from Galen, who, whatever ill use he may have made of the doctrine of " natural faculties," nevertheless had the great merit of perceiving that local forces play a great part in physiology.

The same truth was recognized by Glisson, but it was first prominently brought forward in the Hallerian doctrine of the "vis insita" of muscles. If muscle can contract without nerve, there is an end of the Cartesian mechanical explanation of its contraction by the influx of animal spirits.

The discoveries of Trembley tended in the same direction. In the freshwater *Hydra*, no trace was to be found of that complicated machinery upon which the performance of the functions in the higher animals was supposed to depend. And yet the hydra moved, fed, grew, multiplied, and its fragments, exhibited all the powers of the whole. And, finally, the work of Caspar F. Wolff, (" Theoria Generationis," 1759,) by demonstrating the fact that the growth and development of both plants and animals take place antecedently to the existence of their grosser organs, and are, in fact, the causes and not the consequences of organization (as then understood), sapped the foundations of the Cartesian physiology as a complete expression of vital phenomena.

For Wolff, the physical basis of life is a fluid, possessed of a "vis essentialis " and a " solidescibilitas," in virtue of which it gives rise to organization ; and, as he points out, this conclusion strikes at the root of the whole iatro-mechanical system.

In this country, the great authority of John Hunter exerted a similar influence ; though it must be admitted that the too sibylline utterances which are the outcome of Hunter's struggles to define his conceptions are often susceptible of more than one interpretation. Nevertheless, on some points Hunter is clear enough. For example, he is of opinion that "Spirit is only a property of matter " (" Introduction to Natural History," p. 6), he is prepared to renounce animism (*l. c.* p. 8), and his conception of life is so completely physical that he thinks of it as something which can exist in a state of combination in the food. " The aliment we take in has in it, in a fixed state, the real life ; and this does not become active until it has got into the lungs ; for there it is freed from its prison " (" Observations on Physiology," p. 113). He also thinks that " It is more in accord with the general principles of the animal machine to suppose that none of its effects are produced from any mechanical principle whatever ; and that every effect is produced from an action in the part ; which action is produced by a stimulus upon the part which acts, or upon some other part with which this part sympathizes so as to take up the whole action " (*l. c.* p. 152).

And Hunter is as clear as Wolff, with whose work he was probably unacquainted, that " whatever life is, it most certainly does not depend upon structure or organization " (*l. c.* p. 114).

Of course it is impossible that Hunter could have intended to deny the existence of purely mechanical operations in the animal body. But while, with Borelli and Boerhaave, he looked upon absorption, nutrition, and secretion as operations effected by means of the small vessels, he differed from the mechanical physiologists, who regarded these operations as the result of the mechanical prop-erties of the small vessels, such as the size, form, and disposition of their canals and apertures. Hunter, on the contrary, considers them to be the effect of properties of these vessels which are not mechanical but vital. "The vessels," says he, "have more of the polypus in them than any other part of the body," and he talks of the "living and sensitive principles of the arteries," and even of the "dispositions or feelings of the arteries." "When the blood is good and genuine the sensations of the arteries, or the dispositions for sensation, are agreeable. . . . It is then they dispose of the blood to the best advantage, increasing the growth of the whole, supplying any losses, keeping up a due succession, etc." (*l. c.* p. 133).

If we follow Hunter's conceptions to their logical issue, the life of one of the higher animals is essentially the sum of the lives of all the vessels, each of which is a sort of physiological unit, answering to a polype ; and, as health is the result of the normal "action of the vessels," so is disease an effect of their abnormal action. Hunter thus stands in thought, as in time, midway between Borelli on the one hand, and Bichat on the other.

The acute founder of general anatomy, in fact, outdoes Hunter in his desire to exclude physical reasonings from the realm of life. Except in the interpretation of the action of the sense organs, he will not allow physics to have anything to do with physiology.

"To apply the physical sciences to physiology is to explain the phenomena of living bodies by the law of inert bodies. Now this is a false principle, hence all its consequences are marked with the same stamp. Let us leave to chemistry its affinity ; to physics, its elasticity and its gravity. Let us invoke for physiology only sensibility and contractility." ("Anatomie générale," i. p. liv.)

Of all the unfortunate dicta of men of eminent ability this seems one of the most unhappy, when we think of

what the application of the methods and the data of physics and chemistry has done toward bringing physiology into its present state. It is not too much to say that one half of a modern text-book of physiology consists of applied physics and chemistry ; and that it is exactly in the exploration of the phenomena of sensibility and contractility that physics and chemistry have exerted the most potent influence.

Nevertheless, Bichat rendered a solid service to physiological progress by insisting upon the fact that what we call life, in one of the higher animals, is not an indivisible unitary archæus dominating, from its central seat, the parts of the organism, but a compound result of the synthesis of the separate lives of those parts.

"All animals," says he, "are assemblages of different organs, each of which performs its function and concurs, after its fashion, in the preservation of the whole. They are so many special machines in the general machine which constitutes the individual. But each of these special machines is itself compounded of many tissues of very different natures, which in truth constitute the elements of those organs" (*l. c.* lxxix.). "The conception of a proper vitality is applicable only to these simple tissues and not to the organs themselves" (*l. c.* lxxxiv.).

And Bichat proceeds to make the obvious application of this doctrine of synthetic life, if I may so call it, to pathology. Since diseases are only alterations of vital properties, and the properties of each tissue are distinct from those of the rest, it is evident that the diseases of each tissue must be different from those of the rest. Therefore, in any organ composed of different tissues, one may be diseased and the other remain healthy; and this is what happens in most cases (*l. c.* lxxxv.)

In a spirit of true prophecy, Bichat says, "We have arrived at an epoch, in which pathological anatomy should start afresh." For, as the analysis of the organs had led him to the tissues, as the physiological units of the organism; so, in a succeeding generation, the analysis of the tissues led to the cell as the physiological element of the tissues. The contemporaneous study of development brought out the same result; and the zoologists and botanists, exploring the simplest and the lowest forms of animated beings, confirmed the great induction of the cell theory. Thus the apparently opposed views, which have been battling with one another ever since the middle of the last century, have proved to be each half the earth.

The proposition of Descartes that the body of a living man is a machine, the actions of which are explicable by the known laws of matter and motion, is unquestionably largely true. But it is also true, that the living body is a synthesis of innumerable physiological elements, each of which may nearly be described, in Wolff's words, as a fluid possessed of a " vis essentialis," and a " solidescibilitas "; or, in modern phrase, as protoplasm susceptible of structural metamorphosis and functional metabolism : and that the only machinery, in the precise sense in which the Cartesian school understood mechanism, is that which co-ordinates and regulates these physiological units into an organic whole.

In fact, the body is a machine of the nature of an army, not of that of a watch or of a hydraulic apparatus. Of this army each cell is a soldier, an organ, a brigade, the central nervous system headquarters and field telegraph, the alimentary and circulatory system the commissariat. Losses are made good by recruits born in camp, and the life of the individual is a campaign, conducted successfully for a number of years, but with certain defeat in the long run.

The efficacy of an army, at any given moment, depends on the health of the individual soldier, and on the perfection of the machinery by which he is led and brought into action at the proper time; and, therefore, if the analogy holds good, there can be only

two kinds of diseases, the one dependent on abnormal states of the physiological units, the other on perturbations of their co-ordinating and alimentative machinery.

Hence, the establishment of the cell theory, in normal biology, was swiftly followed by a "cellular pathology," as its logical counterpart. I need not remind you how great an instrument of investigation this doctrine has proved in the hands of the man of genius to whom its development is due, and who would probably be the last to forget that abnormal conditions of the co-ordinative and distributive machinery of the body are no less important factors of disease.

Henceforward, as it appears to me, the connection of medicine with the biological sciences is clearly defined. Pure pathology is that branch of biology which defines the particular perturbation of cell-life, or of the co-ordinating machinery, or of both, on which the phenomena of disease depend.

Those who are conversant with the present state of biology will hardly hesitate to admit that the conception of the life of one of the higher animals as the summation of the lives of a cell aggregate, brought into harmonious action by a co-ordinative machinery formed by some of these cells, constitutes a permanent acquisition of physiological science. But the last form of the battle between the animistic and the physical views of life is seen in the contention whether physical analysis of vital phenomena can be carried beyond this point or not.

There are some to whom living protoplasm is a substance, even such as Harvey conceived the blood to be, "summâ cum providentiâ et intellectu in finem certum agens, quasi ratiocinio quodam;" and who look with as little favor as Bichat did, upon any attempt to apply the principles and the methods of physics and chemistry to the investigation of the vital processes of growth, metabolism, and contractility. They stand upon the ancient ways;

only, in accordance with that progress toward democracy, which a great political writer has declared to be the fatal characteristic of modern times, they substitute a republic formed by a few billion of "animulæ" for the monarchy of the all-pervading "anima."

Others, on the contrary, supported by a robust faith in the universal applicability of the principles laid down by Descartes, and seeing that the actions called "vital" are, so far as we have any means of knowing, nothing but changes of place of particles of matter, look to molecular physics to achieve the analysis of the living protoplasm itself into a molecular mechanism. If there is any truth in the received doctrines of physics, that contrast between living and inert matter, on which Bichat lays so much stress, does not exist. In nature, nothing is at rest, nothing is amorphous; the simplest particle of that which men in their blindness are pleased to call "brute matter" is a vast aggregate of molecular mechanisms performing complicated movements of immense rapidity, and sensitively adjusting themselves to every change in the surrounding world. Living matter differs from other matter in degree and not in kind; the microcosm repeats the macrocosm; and one chain of causation connects the nebulous original of suns and planetary systems with the protoplasmic foundation of life and organization.

From this point of view, pathology is the analogue of the theory of perturbations in astronomy; and therapeutics resolves itself into the discovery of the means by which a system of forces competent to eliminate any given perturbation may be introduced into the economy. And, as pathology bases itself upon normal physiology, so therapeutics rests upon pharmacology; which is, strictly speaking, a part of the great biological topic of the influence of conditions on the living organism, and has no scientific foundation apart from physiology.

It appears to me that there is no more hopeful indication of the progress of medicine toward the ideal of Descartes than is to be derived from a comparison of the state of pharmacology, at the present day, with that which existed forty years ago. If we consider the knowledge positively acquired, in this short time, of the *modus operandi* of urari, of atropia, of physostigmin, of veratria, of casca, of strychnia, of bromide of potassium, of phosphorus, there can surely be no ground for doubting that, sooner or later, the pharmacologist will supply the physician with the means of affecting, in any desired sense, the functions of any physiological element of the body. It will, in short, become possible to introduce into the economy a molecular mechanism which, like a very cunningly-contrived torpedo, shall find its way to some particular group of living elements, and cause an explosion among them, leaving the rest untouched.

The search for the explanation of diseased states in modified cell-life; the discovery of the important part played by parasitic organisms in the ætiology of disease; the elucidation of the action of medicaments by the methods and the data of experimental physiology; appear to me to be the greatest steps which have ever been made toward the establishment of medicine on a scientific basis. I need hardly say they could not have been made except for the advance of normal biology.

There can be no question, then, as to the nature or the value of the connection between medicine and the biological sciences. There can be no doubt that the future of pathology and of therapeutics, and, therefore, that of practical medicine, depends upon the extent to which those who occupy themselves with these subjects are trained in the methods and impregnated with the fundamental truths of biology.

And, in conclusion, I venture to suggest that the collective sagacity of this Congress could occupy itself with no more important question than with this : How is medical education to be arranged, so that, without entangling the student in those details of the systematist which are valueless to him, he may be enabled to obtain a firm grasp of the great truths respecting animal and vegetable life, without which, notwithstanding all the progress of scientific medicine, he will still find himself an empiric ?

III.

JOSEPH PRIESTLEY.

IF the man to perpetuate whose memory we have this day raised a statue had been asked on what part of his busy life's work he set the highest value, he would undoubtedly have pointed to his voluminous contributions to theology. In season and out of season, he was the steadfast champion of that hypothesis respecting the Divine nature which is termed Unitarianism by its friends and Socinianism by its foes. Regardless of odds, he was ready to do battle with all comers in that cause ; and if no adversaries entered the lists, he would sally forth to seek them.

To this, his highest ideal of duty, Joseph Priestley sacrificed the vulgar prizes of life, which, assuredly, were within easy reach of a man of his singular energy and varied abilities. For this object, he put aside, as of secondary importance, those scientific investigations which he loved so well, and in which he showed himself so competent to enlarge the boundaries of natural knowledge and to win fame. In this cause, he not only cheerfully suffered obloquy from the bigoted and the unthinking, and came within sight of martyrdom ; but bore with that which is much harder to be borne than all these, the unfeigned astonishment and hardly disguised contempt of a brilliant society, composed of men whose sympathy and esteem must have been most dear to

him, and to whom it was simply incomprehensible that a philosopher should seriously occupy himself with any form of Christianity.

It appears to me that the man who, setting before himself such an ideal of life, acted up to it consistently, is worthy of the deepest respect, whatever opinion may be entertained as to the real value of the tenets which he so zealously propagated and defended.

But I am sure that I speak not only for myself, but for all this assemblage, when I say that our purpose to-day is to do honor, not to Priestley, the Unitarian divine, but to Priestley, the fearless defender of rational freedom in thought and in action ; to Priestley, the philosophic thinker ; to that Priestley who held a foremost place among " the swift runners who hand over the lamp of life," and transmit from one generation to another the fire kindled, in the childhood of the world, at the Promethean altar of Science.

The main incidents of Priestley's life are so well known that I need dwell upon them at no great length.

Born in 1733, at Fieldhead, near Leeds, and brought up among Calvinists of the straitest orthodoxy, the boy's striking natural ability led to his being devoted to the profession of a minister of religion ; and, in 1752, was sent to the Dissenting Academy at Daventry—an institution which authority left undisturbed, though its existence contravened the law. The teachers under whose instruction and influence the young man came at Daventry, carried out to the letter the injunction to " try all things: hold fast that which is good," and encouraged the discussion of every imaginable proposition with complete freedom, the leading professors taking opposite sides ; a discipline which, admirable as it may be from a purely scientific point of view, would seem to be calculated to make acute, rather than sound, divines. Priestley tells us, in his " Autobiography," that he generally found himself on the unorthodox side : and as he grew older, and his faculties attained their maturity, this native tendency toward heterodoxy grew with his growth and strengthened with his strength. He passed from Calvinism to Arianism; and finally, in middle life, landed in that very broad form of Unitarianism, by which his craving after a credible and consistent theory of things was satisfied.

On leaving Daventry, Priestley became minister of a congregation, first at Needham Market, and secondly at Nantwich; but whether on account of his heterodox opinions, or of the stuttering which impeded his expression of them in the pulpit, little success attended his efforts in this capacity. In 1761, a career much more suited to his abilities became open to him. He was appointed "tutor in the languages" in the Dissenting Academy at Warrington, in which capacity, besides giving three courses of lectures, he taught Latin, Greek, French, and Italian, and read lectures on the Theory of Language and Universal Grammar, on Oratory, Philosophical Criticism, and Civil law. And it is interesting to observe that, as a teacher, he encouraged and cherished in those whom he instructed, the freedom which he had enjoyed, in his own student days, at Daventry. One of his pupils tells us that,

"At the conclusion of his lecture, he always encouraged his students to express their sentiments relative to the subject of it, and to urge any objections to what he had delivered, without reserve. It pleased him when any one commenced such a conversation. In order to excite the freest discussion, he occasionally invited the students to drink tea with him, in order to canvass the subjects of his lectures. I do not recollect that he ever showed the least displeasure at the strongest objections that were made to what he delivered, but I distinctly remember the smile of approbation with which he usually received them; nor did he fail to point out, in a very encouraging manner, the ingenuity or force of any remarks that were made, when they merited these characters. His object, as well as Dr. Aikin's, was to engage the students to examine and decide for themselves, uninfluenced by the sentiments of any other persons." (" Life and Correspondence of Dr. Priestley," by J. T. Rutt. Vol. i. p. 50.)

It would be difficult to give a better description of a model teacher than that conveyed in these words.

From his earliest days, Priestley had shown a strong bent toward the study of nature; and his brother Timothy tells us that the boy put spiders into bottles to see how long they would live in the same air—a curious anticipation of the investigations of his later years. At Nantwich, where he set up a school, Priestley informs us that he bought an air pump, an electrical machine, and other instruments, in the use of which he instructed his scholars. But he does not seem to have devoted himself seriously to physical science until 1766, when he had the great good fortune to meet Benjamin Franklin, whose friendship he ever afterward enjoyed. Encouraged by Franklin, he wrote a " History of Electricity," which was published in 1767, and appears to have met with considerable success.

In the same year, Priestley left Warrington to become the minister of a congregation at Leeds; and, here, happening to live next door to a public brewery, as he says,

"I, at first, amused myself with making experiments on the fixed air which I found ready-made in the process of fermentation. When I removed from that house I was under the necessity of making fixed air for myself; and one experiment leading to another, as I have distinctly and faithfully noted in my various publications on the subject, I by degrees contrived a convenient apparatus for the purpose, but of the cheapest kind.

" When I began these experiments I knew very little of *chemistry*, and had, in a manner, no idea on the subject before I attended a course of chemical lectures, delivered in the Academy at Warrington, by Dr. Turner of Liverpool. But I have often thought that, upon the whole, this circumstance was no disadvantage to me; as, in this situation, I was led to devise an apparatus and processes of my own, adapted to my peculiar views; whereas, if I had been previously accustomed to the usual chemical processes, I should not have so easily thought of any other, and without new modes of operation, I should hardly have discovered anything materially new." (" Autobiography," §§ 100, 101.)

The first outcome of Priestley's chemical work, published in 1772, was of a very practical character. He discovered the way of impregnating water with an excess of " fixed air," or carbonic acid, and thereby producing what we now know as " soda water " —a service to naturally, and still more to artificially, thirsty souls which those whose parched throats and hot heads are cooled by morning draughts of that beverage, cannot too greatfully acknowledge. In the same year, Priestley communicated the extensive series of observations which his industry and ingenuity had accumulated, in the course of four years, to the Royal Society, under the title of " Observations on Different Kinds of Air " —a memoir which was justly regarded of so much merit and importance, that the Society at once conferred upon the author the highest distinction in their power, by awarding him the Copley Medal.

In 1771 a proposal was made to Priestley to accompany Captain Cook in his second voyage to the South Seas. He accepted it, and his congregation agreed to pay an assistant to supply his place during his absence. But the appointment lay in the hands of the Board of Longitude, of which certain clergymen were members ; and whether these worthy ecclesiastics feared that Priestley's presence among the ship's company might expose his Majesty's Sloop *Resolution* to the fate which aforetime befell a certain ship that went from Joppa to Tarshish ; or whether they were alarmed lest a Socinian should undermine that piety which, in the days of Commodore Trunnion, so strikingly characterized sailors, does not appear, but, at any rate, they objected to Priestley " on account of his religious principles," and appointed the two Forsters, whose "religious principles," if they had been known to these well-meaning but not far-sighted persons, would probably have surprised them.

In 1772 another proposal was made to Priestley. Lord Shelburne, desiring a " literary companion," had been brought into communication with Priestley by the good offices of a friend of both, Dr. Price ; and offered him the nominal post of librarian, with a good house and appointments, and an annuity in case of the termination of the engagement. Priestley accepted the offer, and remained with Lord Shelburne for seven years, sometimes residing at Calne, sometimes traveling abroad with the Earl.

Why the connection terminated has never been exactly known ; but it is certain that Lord Shelburne behaved with the utmost consideration and kindness toward Priestley, that he fulfilled his engagements to the letter ; and that, at a later period, he expressed a desire that Priestley should return to his old footing in his house. Probably enough, the politician, aspiring to the highest offices in the state, may have found the position of the protector of a man who was being denounced all over the country as an infidel and an atheist somewhat embarrassing. In fact, a passage in Priestley's " Autobiography" on the occasion of the publication of his " Disquisitions relating to Matter and Spirit," which took place in 1777, indicates pretty clearly the state of the case :—

" (126) It being probable that this publication would be unpopular, and might be the means of bringing odium on my patron, several attempts were made by his friends, though none by himself, to dissuade me from persisting in it. But being, as I thought, engaged in the cause of important truth, I proceeded without regard to any consequences, assuring them that this publication should not be injurious to his lordship."

It is not unreasonable to suppose that his lordship, as a keen, practical man of the world, did not derive much satisfaction from this assurance. The "evident marks of dissatisfaction " which Priestley says he first perceived in his patron in 1778, may well have arisen from the peer's not unnatural uneasiness as to what his domesticated, but not tamed, philosopher might write next, and what storm might thereby be brought down on his own head ; and it speaks very highly for Lord Shelburne's delicacy that, in the midst of such perplexities, he made not the least attempt to interfere with Priestley's freedom of action. In 1780, however, he intimated to Dr. Price that he should be glad to establish Priestley on his Irish estates: the suggestion was interpreted, as Lord Shelburne probably intended it should be, and Priestley left him, the annuity of £150 a year, which had been promised in view of such a contingency, being punctually paid.

After leaving Calne, Priestley spent some little time in London, and then, having settled in Birmingham at the desire of his brother-in-law, he was soon invited to become the minister of a large congregation. This settlement Priestley considered, at the time, to be "the happiest event of his life." And well he might think so; for it gave him competence and leisure; placed him within reach of the best makers of apparatus of the day; made him a member of that remarkable "Lunar Society," at whose meetings he could exchange thoughts with such men as Watt, Wedgewood, Darwin, and Boulton; and threw open to him the pleasant house of the Galtons at Barr, where these men, and others of less note, formed a society of exceptional charm and intelligence.*

But these halcyon days were ended by a bitter storm. The French Rev-

olution broke out. An electric shock ran through the nations; whatever there was of corrupt and retrograde, and at the same time, a great deal of what there was of best and noblest, in European society shuddered at the outburst of long-pent-up social fires. Men's feelings were excited in a way that we, in this generation, can hardly comprehend. Party wrath and virulence were expressed in a manner unparalleled, and it is to be hoped impossible, in our times; and Priestley and his friends were held up to public scorn, even in Parliament, as fomenters of sedition. A "Church-and-King" cry was raised against the Liberal Dissenters; and, in Birmingham, it was intensified and specially directed toward Priestley by a local controversy, in which he had engaged with his usual vigor. In 1791, the celebration of the second anniversary of the taking of the Bastille by a public dinner, with which Priestley had nothing whatever to do, gave the signal to the loyal and pious mob, who, unchecked, and indeed to some extent encouraged, by those who were responsible for order, had the town at their mercy for three days. The chapels and houses of the leading Dissenters were wrecked, and Priestley and his family had to fly for their lives, leaving library, apparatus, papers, and all their possessions, a prey to the flames.

Priestley never returned to Birmingham. He bore the outrages and losses inflicted upon him with extreme patience and sweetness,* and betook himself to London. But even his scientific colleagues gave him a cold shoulder; and though he was elected minister of a congregation at Hackney, he felt his position to be insecure, and finally determined on emigrating to the United States. He

---

* See "The Life of Mary Anne Schimmelpenninck." Mrs. Schimmelpenninck (née Galton) remembered Priestley very well, and her description of him is worth quotation:—"A man of admirable simplicity, gentleness and kindness of heart, united with great acuteness of intellect. I can never forget the impression produced on me by the serene expression of his countenance. He, indeed, seemed present with God by recollection, and with man by cheerfulness. I remember that, in the assembly of these distinguished men, among whom Mr. Boulton, by his noble manner, his fine countenance (which much resembled that of Louis XIV.), and princely munificence, stood pre-eminently as the great Mecænas; even as a child, I used to feel, when Dr. Priestley entered after him, that the glory of the one was terrestrial, that of the other celestial; and utterly far as I am removed from a belief in the sufficiency of Dr. Priestley's theological creed, I cannot but here record this evidence of the eternal power of any portion of the truth held in its vitality."

---

* Even Mrs. Priestley, who might be forgiven for regarding the destroyers of her household gods with some asperity, contents herself, in writing to Mrs. Barbauld, with the sarcasm that the Birmingham people "will scarcely find so many respectable characters, a second time, to make a bonfire of."

landed in America in 1794; lived quietly with his sons at Northumberland, in Pennsylvania, where his posterity still flourished; and, clearheaded and busy to the last, died on the 6th of February, 1804.

Such were the conditions under which Joseph Priestley did the work which lay before him, and then, as the Norse Sagas say, went out of the story. The work itself was of the most varied kind. No human interest was without its attraction for Priestley, and few men have ever had so many irons in the fire at once; but, though he may have burned his fingers a little, very few who have tried that operation have burned their fingers so little. He made admirable discoveries in science; his philosophical treatises are still well worth reading; his political works are full of insight and replete with the spirit of freedom; and while all these sparks flew off from his anvil, the controversial hammer rained a hail of blows on orthodox priest and bishop. While thus engaged, the kindly, cheerful doctor felt no more wrath or uncharitableness toward his opponents than a smith does toward his iron. But if the iron could only speak!—and the priests and bishops took the point of view of the iron.

No doubt what Priestley's friends repeatedly urged upon him—that he would have escaped the heavier trials of his life and done more for the advancement of knowledge, if he had confined himself to his scientific pursuits and let his fellow-men go their way—was true. But it seems to have been Priestley's feeling that he was a man and a citizen before he was a philosopher, and that the duties of the two former positions are at least as imperative as those of the latter. Moreover, there are men (and I think Priestley was one of them) to whom the satisfaction of throwing down a triumphant fallacy is as great as that which attends the discovery of a new truth; who feel better satisfied with the government of the world, when they have been helping Providence by knocking an imposture on the head; and who care even more for freedom of thought than for mere advance of knowledge. These men are the Carnots who organize victory for truth, and they are, at least, as important as the generals who visibly fight her battles in the field.

Priestley's reputation as a man of science rests upon his numerous and important contributions to the chemistry of gaseous bodies; and to form a just estimate of the value of his work—of the extent to which it advanced the knowledge of fact and the development of sound theoretical views—we must reflect what chemistry was in the first half of the eighteenth century.

The vast science which now passes under that name had no existence. Air, water, and fire were still counted among the elemental bodies; and though Van Helmont, a century before, had distinguished different kinds of air as *gas ventosum* and *gas sylvestre*, and Boyle and Hales had experimentally defined the physical properties of air, and discriminated some of the various kinds of aëriform bodies, no one suspected the existence of the numerous totally distinct gaseous elements which are now known, or dreamed that the air we breathe and the water we drink are compounds of gaseous elements.

But, in 1754, a young Scotch physician, Dr. Blank, made the first clearing in this tangled backwood of knowledge. And it gives one a wonderful impression of the juvenility of scientific chemistry to think that Lord Brougham, whom so many of us recollect, attended Black's lectures when he was a student in Edinburgh. Black's researches gave the world the novel and startling conception of a gas that was a permanently elastic fluid like air, but that differed from common air in being much heavier, very poisonous, and in having the properties of an acid, capable of neutralizing the strongest alkalies; and it took the world some time to become accustomed to the notion.

A dozen years later, one of the most sagacious and accurate investigators who has adorned this, or any other, country, Henry Cavendish, published a memoir in the " Philosophical Transactions," in which he deals not only with the " fixed air " (now called carbonic acid or carbonic anhydride) of Black, but with " inflammable air," or what we now term hydrogen.

By the rigorous application of weight and measure to all his processes, Cavendish implied the belief subsequently formulated by Lavoisier, that, in chemical processes, matter is neither created nor destroyed, and indicated the path along which all future explorers must travel. Nor did he himself halt until this path led him, in 1784, to the brilliant and fundamental discovery that water is composed of two gases united in fixed and constant proportions.

It is a trying ordeal for any man to be compared with Black and Cavendish, and Priestley cannot be said to stand on their level. Nevertheless, his achievements are not only great in themselves, but truly wonderful, if we consider the disadvantages under which he labored. Without the careful scientific training of Black, without the leisure and appliances secured by the wealth of Cavendish, he scaled the walls of science as so many Englishmen have done before and since his day; and trusting to mother wit to supply the place of training, and to ingenuity to create apparatus out of washing tubs, he discovered more new gases than all his predecessors put together had done. He laid the foundations of gas analysis; he discovered the complementary actions of animal and vegetable life upon the constituents of the atmosphere; and, finally, he crowned his work, this day one hundred years ago, by the discovery of that "pure dephlogisticated air " to which the French chemists subsequently gave the name of oxygen. Its importance, as the constituent of the atmosphere which disappears in the processes of respiration and combustion, and is re-

stored by green plants growing in sunshine, was proved somewhat later. For these brilliant discoveries, the Royal Society elected Priestley a fellow and gave him their medal, while the Academies of Paris and St. Petersburg conferred their membership upon him. Edinburgh had made him an honorary doctor of laws at an early period of his career; but, I need hardly add, that a man of Priestley's opinions received no recognition from the universities of his own country.

That Priestley's contributions to the knowledge of chemical fact were of the greatest importance, and that they richly deserve all the praise that has been awarded to them, is unquestionable; but it must, at the same time, be admitted that he had no comprehension of the deeper significance of his work; and, so far from contributing anything to the theory of the facts which he discovered, or assisting in their rational explanation, his influence to the end of his life was warmly exerted in favor of error. From first to last, he was a stiff adherent of the phlogiston doctrine which was prevalent when his studies commenced; and, by a curious irony of fate, the man who by the discovery of what he called " dephlogisticated air " furnished the essential datum for the true theory of combustion, of respiration, and of the composition of water, to the end of his days fought against the inevitable corollaries from his own labors. His last scientific work, published in 1800, bears the title, " The Doctrine of Phlogiston established, and that of the Composition of Water refuted."

When Priestley commenced his studies, the current belief was, that atmospheric air, freed from accidental impurities, is a simple elementary substance, indestructible and unalterable, as water was supposed to be. When a combustible burned, or when an animal breathed in air, it was supposed that a substance, " phlogiston," the matter of heat and light, passed from the burning or breathing body into it, and destroyed its powers of supporting life and combustion. Thus, air contained in a vessel in which a lighted candle had gone out, or a living animal had breathed until it could breath no longer, was called "phlogisticated." The same result was supposed to be brought about by the addition of what Priestley called "nitrous gas" to common air.

In the course of his researches, Priestley found that the quantity of common air which can thus become "phlogisticated," amounts to about one-fifth the volume of the whole quantity submitted to experiment. Hence it appeared that common air consists, to the extent of four-fifths of its volume, of air which is already "phlogisticated;" while the other fifth is free from phlogiston, or "dephlogisticated." On the other hand, Priestley found that air "phlogisticated" by combustion or respiration could be "dephlogisticated," or have the properties of pure common air restored to it, by the action of green plants in sunshine. The question, therefore, would naturally arise— as common air can be wholly phlogisticated by combustion, and converted into a substance which will no longer support combustion, is it possible to get air that shall be less phlogisticated than common air, and consequently support combustion better than common air does?

Now, Priestley says that, in 1774, the possibility of obtaining air less phlogisticated than common air had not occurred to him. ("Experiments and Observations on Different Kinds of Air, vol. ii. p. 31.) But in pursuing his experiments on the evolution of air from various bodies by means of heat, it happened that, on the 1st of August, 1774, he threw the heat of the sun, by means of a large burning glass which he had recently obtained, upon a substance which was then called *mercurius calcinatus per se*, and which is commonly known as red precipitate.

"I presently found that, by means of this lens, air was expelled from it very readily.

Having got about three or four times as much as the bulk of my materials, I admitted water to it, and found that it was not imbibed by it. But what surprised me more than I can well express, was that a candle burned in this air with a remarkably vigorous flame, very much like that enlarged flame with which a candle burns in nitrous air, exposed to iron or lime of sulphur; but as I had got nothing like this remarkable appearance from any kind of air besides this particular modification of nitrous air, and I knew no nitrous acid was used in the preparation of *mercurius calcinatus* I was utterly at a loss how to account for it.

"In this case also, though I did not give sufficient attention to the circumstance at that time, the flame of the candle, besides being larger, burned with more splendor and heat than in that species of nitrous air; and a piece of red-hot wood sparkled in it, exactly like paper dipped in a solution of nitre, and it consumed very fast—an experiment which I had never thought of trying with nitrous air." (*Ibid.* pp. 34, 35).

Priestley obtained the same sort of air from red lead, but, as he says himself, he remained in ignorance of the properties of this new kind of air for seven months, or until March, 1775, when he found that the new air behaved with "nitrous gas" in the same way as the dephlogisticated part of common air does; * but that, instead of being diminished to four-fifths, it almost completely vanished, and, therefore, showed itself to be "between five and six times as good as the best common air I have ever met with." (*Ibid.* p. 48.) As this new air thus appeared to be completely free from phlogiston, Priestley called it "dephlogisticated air."

What was the nature of this air? Priestley found that the same kind of air was to be obtained by moistening with the spirit of niter (which he terms nitrous acid) any kind of earth that is free from phlogiston, and applying heat; and consequently he says: "There remained no doubt on my mind but that the atmospherical air, or the thing that we breathe, consists of the nitrous acid and earth, with so much pholgiston as is necessary to its elasticity, and likewise so much more as is required to bring it from

* "Experiments and Observations on Different Kinds of Air," vol. ii. p. 40.

its state of perfect purity to the mean condition in which we find it." (*Ibid.* p. 55.)

Priestley's view, in fact, is that atmospheric air is a kind of saltpetre, in which the potash is replaced by some unknown earth. And in speculating on the manner in which saltpetre is formed, he enunciates the hypothesis "that niter is formed by a real *decomposition of the air itself*, the *bases* that are presented to it having, in such circumstances, a nearer affinity with the spirit of niter than that kind of earth with which it is united in the atmosphere." (*Ibid.* p. 60. The italics are Priestley's own.)

It would have heen hard for the most ingenious person to have wandered farther from the truth than Priestley does in this hypothesis; and, though Lavoisier undoubtedly treated Priestley very ill, and pretended to have discovered dephlogisticated air, or oxygen, as he called it, independently, we can almost forgive him, when we reflect how different were the ideas which the great French chemist attached to the body which Priestley discovered.

They are like two navigators of whom the first sees a new country, but takes clouds for mountains and mirage for lowlands; while the second determines its length and breadth, and lays down on a chart its exact place, so that, thenceforth, it serves as a guide to his successors, and becomes a secure outpost whence new explorations may be pushed.

Nevertheless, as Priestley himself somewhere remarks, the first object of physical science is to ascertain facts, and the service which he rendered to chemistry by the definite establishment of a large number of new and fundamentally important facts, is such as to entitle him to a very high place among the fathers of chemical science.

It is difficult to say whether Priestley's philosophical, political, or theological views were most responsi-

ble for the bitter hatred which was borne to him by a large body of his countrymen,* and which found its expression in the malignant insinuations in which Burke, to his everlasting shame, indulged in the House of Commons.

Without containing much that will be new to the readers of Hobbes, Spinoza, Collins, Hume, and Hartley, and, indeed, while making no pretensions to originality, Priestley's " Disquisitions relating to Matter and Spirit," and his " Doctrine of Philosophical Necessity illustrated," are among the most powerful, clear, and unflinching expositions of materialism and necessarianism which exist in the English language, and are still well worth reading.

Priestley denied the freedom of the will in the sense of its self-determination; he denied the existence of a soul distinct from the body; and as a natural consequence, he denied the natural immortality of man.

In relation to these matters English opinion, a century ago, was very much what it is now.

A man may be a necessarian without incurring graver reproach than that implied in being called a gloomy fanatic, necessarianism, though very shocking, having a note of Calvinistic orthodoxy; but, if a man is a materialist; or, if good authorities say he is and must be so, in spite of his assertion to the contrary; or, if he acknowl-

---

* " In all the newspapers and most of the periodical publications I was represented as an unbeliever in Revelation, and no better than an atheist."—" Autobiography," Rutt. vol. i. p. 124. " On the walls of houses, etc., and especially where I usually went, were to be seen, in large characters, 'MADAN FOREVER; DAMN PRIESTLEY; NO PRESBYTERIANISM; DAMN THE PRESBYTERIANS,' etc., etc.; and, at one time, I was followed by a number of boys, who left their play, repeating what they had seen on the walls, and shouting out, ' *Damn Priestley; damn him, damn him, forever, forever*,' etc., etc. This was no doubt a lesson which they had been taught by their parents, and what they, I fear, had learned from their superiors."—" Appeal to the Public on the Subject of the Riots at Birmingham."

edge himself unable to see good reasons for believing in the natural immortality of man, respectable folks look upon him as an unsafe neighbor of a cash-box, as an actual or potential sensualist, the more virtuous in outward seeming, the more certainly loaded with secret "grave personal sins."

Nevertheless, it is as certain as anything can be, that Joseph Priestley was no gloomy fanatic, but as cheerful and kindly a soul as ever breathed, the idol of children; a man who was hated only by those who did not know him, and who charmed away the bitterest prejudices in personal intercourse; a man who never lost a friend, and the best testimony to whose worth is the generous and tender warmth with which his many friends vied with one another in rendering him substantial help, in all the crises of his career.

The unspotted purity of Priestley's life, the strictness of his performance of every duty, his transparent sincerity, the unostentatious and deep-seated piety which breathes through all his correspondence, are in themselves a sufficient refutation of the hypothesis invented by bigots to cover uncharitableness, that such opinions as his must arise from moral defects. And his statue will do as good service as the brazen image that was set upon a pole before the Israelites, if those who have been bitten by the fiery serpents of sectarian hatred, which still haunt this wilderness of a world, are made whole by looking upon the image of a heretic, who was yet a saint.

Though Priestley did not believe in the natural immortality of man, he held with an almost naïve realism, that man would be raised from the dead by a direct exertion of the power of God, and thenceforward be immortal. And it may be as well for those who may be shocked by this doctrine to know that views, substantially identical with Priestley's, have been advocated, since his time, by two prelates of the Anglican Church: by Dr. Whately, Archbishop of Dublin, in his well-known "Essays;" * and by Dr. Courtenay, Bishop of Kingston in Jamaica, the first edition of whose remarkable book "On the Future States," dedicated to Archbishop Whately, was published in 1843 and the second in 1857. According to Bishop Courtenay,

"The death of the body will cause a cessation of all the activity of the mind by way of natural consequence; to continue forever UNLESS the Creator should interfere."

And again:—

"The natural end of human existence is the 'first death,' the dreamless slumber of the grave, wherein man lies spellbound, soul and body, under the dominion of sin and death—that whatever modes of conscious existence, whatever future states of 'life' or of 'torment' beyond Hades are reserved for man, are results of our blessed Lord's victory over sin and death; that the resurrection of the dead must be preliminary to their entrance into either of the future states, and that the nature and even existence of these states and even the mere fact that there is a futurity of consciousness, can be known *only* through God's revelation of Himself in the Person and the Gospel of His Son."—P. 389.

And now hear Priestley:—

"Man, according to this system (of materialism), is no more than we now see of him. His being commences at the time of his conception, or perhaps at an earlier period. The corporeal and mental faculties, in being in the same substance, grow, ripen, and decay together; and whenever the system is dissolved it continues in a state of dissolution till it shall please that Almighty Being who called it into existence to restore it to life again."—"Matter and Spirit," p. 49.

And again:—

"The doctrine of the Scripture is, that God made man of the dust of the ground, and by simply animating this organized matter, made man that living percipient and intelligent being that he is. According to Revelation, *death* is a state of rest and insensibility, and our only though sure hope of a future life is founded on the doctrine of the resurrection of the whole man at some distant period; this assurance being sufficently confirmed to us both by the evident tokens of a Divine

---

* First series. "On Some of the Peculiarities of the Christian Religion." Essay I. Revelation of a Future State.

commission attending the persons who delivered the doctrine, and especially by the actual resurrection of Jesus Christ, which is more authentically attested than any other fact in history."—*Ibid.*, p. 247.

We all know that "a saint in crape is twice a saint in lawn ; " but it is not yet admitted that the views which are consistent with such saintliness in lawn, become diabolical when held by a mere dissenter.*

I am not here either to defend or to attack Priestley's philosophical views, and I cannot say that I am personally disposed to attach much value to episcopal authority in philosophical questions; but it seems right to call attention to the fact, that those of Priestley's opinions which have brought most odium upon him, have been openly promulgated, without challenge, by persons occupying the highest positions in the State Church.

I must confess that what interests me most about Priestley's materialism, is the evidence that he saw dimly the seed of destruction which such materialism carries within its own bosom. In the course of his reading for his "History of Discoveries relating to Vision, Light, and Colors," he had come upon the speculations of Boscovich and Michell and had been led to admit the sufficiently obvious truth that our knowledge of matter is a knowledge of its properties; and that of its substance—if it have a substance—we know nothing. And this led to the further admission that, so

far as we can know, there may be no difference between the substance of matter and the substance of spirit (" Disquisitions," p. 16). A step farther would have shown Priestley that his materialism was, essentially, very little different from the Idealism of his contemporary, the Bishop of Cloyne.

As Priestley's philosophy is mainly a clear statement of the views of the deeper thinkers of his day, so are his political conceptions based upon those of Locke. Locke's aphorism that "the end of government is the good of mankind," is thus expanded by Priestley :—

" It must necessarily be understood, therefore, whether it be expressed or not, that all people live in society for their mutual advantage; so that the good and happiness of the members, that is, of the majority of the members, of any state, is the great standard by which everything relating to that state must finally be determined." ("Essay on the First Principles of Government." Second edition, 1771, p. 13.)

The little sentence here interpolated, "that is, of the majority of the members of any state," appears to be that passage which suggested to Bentham, according to his own acknowledgment, the famous "greatest happiness" formula, which by substituting "happiness" for "good," has converted a noble into an ignoble principle. But I do not call to mind that there is any utterance in Locke quite so outspoken as the following passage in the " Essay on the First Principles of Government." After laying down as "a fundamental maxim in all governments," the proposition that " kings, senators, and nobles " are " the servants of the public," Priestley goes on to say :—

" But in the largest states, if the abuses of the government should at any time be great and manifest; if the servants of the people, forgetting their masters and their masters' interest, should pursue a separate one of their own; if, instead of considering that they are made for the people, they should consider the people as made for them; if the oppressions and violation of right should be great, flagrant, and universally resented ; if

*Not only is Priestley at one with Bishop Courtenay in this matter, but with Hartley and Bonnet, both of them stout champions of Christianity. Moreover, Archbishop Whately's essay is little better than an expansion of the first paragraph of Hume's famous essay on the Immortality of the Soul :—" By the mere light of reason it seems difficult to prove the immortality of the soul; the arguments for it are commonly derived either from metaphysical topics, or moral, or physical. But it is in reality the Gospel, and the Gospel alone, that has brought *life and immortality to light.*" It is impossible to imagine that a man of Whately's tastes and acquirements had not read Hume or Hartley, though he refers to neither.

the tyrannical governors should have no friends but a few sycophants, who had long preyed upon the vitals of their fellow-citizens, and who might be expected to desert a government whenever their interests should be detached from it; if in consequence of these circumstances, it should become manifest that the risk which would be run in attempting a revolution would be trifling, and the evils which might be apprehended from it were far less than those which were actually suffered and which were daily increasing; in the name of God, I ask, what principles are those which ought to restrain an injured and insulted people from asserting their natural rights, and from changing or even punishing their governors—that is, their servants—who had abused their trust, or from altering the whole form of their government, if it appeared to be of a structure so liable to abuse ? "

As a Dissenter, subject to the operation of the Corporation and Test Acts, and as a Unitarian, excluded from the benefit of the Toleration Act, it is not surprising to find that Priestley had very definite opinions about Ecclesiastical Establishments; the only wonder is that these opinions were so moderate as the following passages show them to have been :—

"Ecclesiastical authority may have been necessary in the infant state of society, and, for the same reason, it may perhaps continue to be, in some degree, necessary as long as society is imperfect; and therefore may not be entirely abolished till civil governments have arrived at a much greater degree of perfection. If, therefore, I were asked whether I should approve of the immediate dissolution of all the ecclesiastical establishments in Europe, I should answer, No. . . Let experiment be first made of *alterations*, or, which is the same thing, of *better establishments* than the present. Let them be reformed in many essential articles, and then not thrown aside entirely till it be found by experience that no good can be made of them."

Priestley goes on to suggest four such reforms of a capital nature :—

" 1. Let the Articles of Faith to be subscribed by candidates for the ministry be greatly reduced. In the formulary of the Church of England, might not thirty-eight out of the thirty-nine be very well spared ? It is a reproach to any Christian establishment if every man cannot claim the benefit of it who can say that he believes in the religion of Jesus Christ as it is set forth in the New Testament. You say the terms are so general that even Deists would quibble and in-

sinuate themselves. I answer that all the articles which are subscribed at present, by no means exclude Deists who will prevaricate; and upon this scheme you would at least exclude fewer honest men."*

The second reform suggested is the equalization, in proportion to work done, of the stipends of the clergy; the third, the exclusion of the bishops from Parliament; and the fourth, complete toleration, so that every man may enjoy the rights of a citizen, and be qualified to serve his country, whether he belong to the Established Church or not.

Opinions such as those I have quoted, respecting the duties and the responsibilities of governors, are the commonplaces of modern Liberalism; and Priestley's views on Ecclesiastical Establishments would, I fear, meet with but a cool reception, as altogether too conservative, from a large proportion of the lineal descendants of the people who taught their children to cry " Damn Priestley ; " and, with that love for the practical application of science which is the source of the greatness of Birmingham, tried to set fire to the doctor's house with sparks from his own electrical machine ; thereby giving the man they called an incendiary and raiser of sedition against Church and King, an appropriately experimental illustration of the nature of arson and riot.

If I have succeeded in putting before you the main features of Priestley's work, its value will become apparent, when we compare the condition of the English nation, as he knew it, with its present state.

The fact that France has been for eighty-five years trying, without much success, to right herself after the great storm of the Revolution, is not unfrequently cited among us, as an indication of some inherent incapacity for self-government among the French people. I think, however, that Englishmen who argue thus, forget that, from the meeting of the

* "Utility of Establishments," in " Essay on First Principles of Government," p. 198, 1771.

Long Parliament in 1640, to the last Stuart rebellion in 1745, is a hundred and five years, and that, in the middle of the last century, we had but just safely freed ourselves from our Bourbons and all that they represented. The corruption of our state was as bad as that of the Second Empire. Bribery was the instrument of government, and peculation its reward. Four-fifths of the seats in the House of Commons were more or less openly dealt with as property. A minister had to consider the state of the vote market, and the sovereign secured a sufficiency of "king's friends" by payments allotted with retail, rather than royal, sagacity.

Barefaced and brutal immorality and intemperance pervaded the land, from the highest to the lowest classes of society. The Established Church was torpid, so far as it was not a scandal ; but those who dissented from it came within the meshes of the Act of Uniformity, the Test Act, and the Corporation Act. By law, such a man as Priestley, being a Unitarian, could neither teach nor preach, and was liable to ruinous fines and long imprisonment.* In those days, the guns that were pointed by the Church against the Dissenters were shotted. The law was a cesspool of iniquity and cruelty. Adam Smith was a new prophet whom few regarded, and commerce was hampered by idiotic impediments, and ruined by still more absurd help, on the part of government.

Birmingham, though already the center of a considerable industry, was a mere village as compared with its present extent. People who traveled went about armed, by reason of the abundance of highwaymen and the paucity and inefficiency of the police. Stage coaches had not reached Birmingham, and it took three days to get to London. Even canals were a recent and much opposed invention.

* In 1732 Doddridge was cited for teaching without the Bishop's leave, at Northampton.

Newton had laid the foundation of a mechanical conception of the physical universe : Hartley, putting a modern face upon ancient materialism, had extended that mechanical conception to psychology ; Linnæus and Haller were beginning to introduce method and order into the chaotic accumulation of biological facts. But those parts of physical science which deal with heat, electricity, and magnetism, and above all, chemistry, in the modern sense, can hardly be said to have had an existence. No one knew that two of the old elemental bodies, air and water, are compounds, and that a third, fire, is not a substance but a motion. The great industries that have grown out of the applications of modern scientific discoveries had no existence, and the man who should have foretold their coming into being in the days of his son, would have been regarded as a mad enthusiast.

In common with many other excellent persons, Priestley believed that man is capable of reaching, and will eventually attain, perfection. If the temperature of space presented no obstacle, I should be glad to entertain the same idea ; but judging from the past progress of our species, I am afraid that the globe will have cooled down so far, before the advent of this natural millennium, that we shall be, at best, perfected Esquimaux. For all practical purposes, however, it is enough that man may visibly improve his condition in the course of a century or so. And, if the picture of the state of things in Priestley's time, which I have just drawn, have any pretense to accuracy, I think it must be admitted that there has been a considerable change for the better.

I need not advert to the well-worn topic of material advancement, in a place in which the very stones testify to that progress—in the town of Watt and of Boulton, I will only remark, in passing, that material advancement has its share in moral and intellectual progress. Becky Sharp's acute remark that it is not difficult to be virtuous on ten thousand a year, has its application to nations; and it is futile to expect a hungry and squalid population to be anything but violent and gross. But as regards other than material welfare, although perfection is not yet in sight—even from the masthead—it is surely true that things are much better than they were.

Take the upper and middle classes as a whole, and it may be said that open immorality and gross intemperance have vanished. Four and six bottle men are as extinct as the dodo. Women of good repute do not gamble, and talk modeled upon Dean Swift's " Art of Polite Conversation " would be tolerated in no decent kitchen.

Members of the legislature are not to be bought ; and constituents are awakening to the fact that votes must not be sold—even for such trifles as rabbits and tea and cake. Political power has passed into the hands of the masses of the people. Those whom Priestley calls their servants have recognized their position, and have requested the master to be so good as to go to school and fit himself for the administration of his property. No civil disability attaches to any one on theological grounds, and the highest offices of the state are open to Papist, Jew, or Secularist.

Whatever men's opinions as to the policy of Establishment, no one can hesitate to admit that the clergy of the Church are men of pure life and conversation, zealous in the discharge of their duties ; and, at present, apparently, more bent on prosecuting one another than on meddling with Dissenters. Theology itself has broadened so much, that Anglican divines put forward doctrines more liberal than those of Priestley ; and, in our state-supported churches, one listener may hear a sermon to which Bossuet might have given his approbation, while another may hear a discourse in which Socrates would find nothing new.

But great as these changes may be, they sink into insignificance beside the progress of physical science, whether we consider the improve-

ment of methods of investigation, or the increase in bulk of solid knowledge. Consider that the labors of Laplace, of Young, of Davy, and of Faraday ; of Cuvier, of Lamarck, and of Robert Brown ; of Von Baer, and of Schwann ; of Smith and of Hutton, have all been carried on since Priestley discovered oxygen ; and consider that they are now things of the past, concealed by the industry of those who have built upon them, as the first founders of a coral reef are hidden beneath the life's work of their successors ; consider that the methods of physical science are slowly spreading into all investigations, and that proofs as valid as those required by her canons of investigation, are being demanded of all doctrines which ask for men's assent ; and you will have a faint image of the astounding difference in this respect between the nineteenth century and the eighteenth.

If we ask what is the deeper meaning of all these vast changes, I think there can be but one reply. They mean that reason has asserted and exercised her primacy over all provinces of human activity : that ecclesiastical authority has been relegated to its proper place ; that the good of the governed has been finally recognized as the end of government, and the complete responsibility of governors to the people as its means ; and that the dependence of natural phenomena in general, on the laws of action of what we call matter has become an axiom.

But it was to bring these things about, and to enforce the recognition of these truths, that Joseph Priestley labored. If the nineteenth century is other and better than the eighteenth, it is, in great measure, to him and to such men as he, that we owe the change. If the twentieth century is to be better than the nineteenth, it will be because there are among us men who walk in Priestley's footsteps.

Such men are not those whom their own generation delights to honor ; such men, in fact, rarely trouble themselves about honor, but ask, in another spirit than Falstaff's, "What is honor? Who hath it? He that died o' Wednesday." But whether Priestley's lot be theirs, and a future generation, in justice and in gratitude, set up their statues; or whether their names and fame are blotted out from remembrance, their work will live as long as time endures. To all eternity, the sun of truth and right will have been increased by their means; to all eternity, falsehood and injustice will be the weaker because they have lived.

IV.

ON SENSATION AND THE UNITY OF STRUCTURE OF SENSIFEROUS ORGANS.*

THE maxim that metaphysical inquiries are barren of result, and that the serious occupation of the mind with them is a mere waste of time and labor, finds much favor in the eyes of the many persons who pride themselves on the possession of sound common sense; and we sometimes hear it enunciated by weighty authorities, as if its natural consequence, the suppression of such studies, had the force of a moral obligation.

In this case, however, as in some others, those who lay down the law seem to forget that a wise legislator will consider, not merely whether his proposed enactment is desirable, but whether obedience to it is possible. For, if the latter question is answered negatively, the former is surely hardly worth debate.

Here, in fact, lies the pith of the reply to those who would make metaphysics contraband of intellect. Whether it is desirable to place a prohibitory duty upon philosophical speculations or not, it is utterly impossible to prevent the importation of them into the mind. And it is not a little curious to observe that those

who most loudly profess to abstain from such commodities are, all the while, unconscious consumers, on a great scale, of one or other of their multitudinous disguises or adulterations. With mouths full of the particular kind of heavily buttered toast which they affect, they inveigh against the eating of plain bread. In truth, the attempt to nourish the human intellect upon a diet which contains no metaphysics is about as hopeful as that of certain Eastern sages to nourish their bodies without destroying life. Everybody has heard the story of the pitiless microscopist, who ruined the peace of mind of one of these mild enthusiasts by showing him the animals moving in a drop of the water with which, in the innocency of his heart, he slaked his thirst; and the unsuspecting devotee of plain common sense may look for as unexpected a shock when the magnifier of severe logic reveals the germs, if not the full-grown shapes, of lively metaphysical postulates rampant amidst his most positive and matter-of-fact notions.

By way of escape from the metaphysical Will-o'-the-wisps generated in the marshes of literature and theology, the serious student is sometimes bidden to betake himself to the solid ground of physical science. But the fish of immortal memory, who threw himself out of the frying-pan into the fire, was not more ill advised than the man who seeks sanctuary from philosophical persecution within the walls of the observatory or of the laboratory. It is said that "metaphysics" owe their name to the fact that, in Aristotle's works, questions of pure philosophy are dealt with immediately after those of physics. If so, the accident is happily symbolical of the essential relations of things; for metaphysical speculation follows as closely upon physical theory as black care upon the horseman.

One need but mention such fundamental, and indeed indispensable, conceptions of the natural philosopher

* Address at the Royal Institution, London, 1880.

as those of atoms and forces : or that of attraction considered as action at a distance ; or that of potential energy ; or the antinomies of a vacuum and a plenum ; to call to mind the metaphysical background of physics and chemistry ; while, in the biological sciences, the case is still worse. What is an individual among the lower plants and animals? Are genera and species realities or abstractions? Is there such a thing as Vital Force? or does the name denote a mere relic of metaphysical fetichism? Is the doctrine of final causes legitimate or illegitimate? These are a few of the metaphysical topics which are suggested by the most elementary study of biological facts. But, more than this, it may be truly said that the roots of every system of philosophy lie deep among the facts of physiology. No one can doubt that the organs and the functions of sensation are as much a part of the province of the physiologist, as are the organs and functions of motion, or those of digestion ; and yet it is impossible to gain an acquaintance with even the rudiments of the physiology of sensation without being led straight to one of the most fundamental of all metaphysical problems. In fact, the sensory operations have been, from time immemorial, the battle-ground of philosophers.

I have more than once taken occasion to point out that we are indebted to Descartes, who happened to be a physiologist as well as a philosopher, for the first distinct enunciation of the essential elements of the true theory of sensation. In later times, it is not to the works of the philosophers, if Hartley and James Mill are excepted, but to those of the physiologists, that we must turn for an adequate account of the sensory process. Haller's luminous, though summary, account of sensation in his admirable " Primæ Lineæ," the first edition of which was printed in 1747, offers a striking contrast to the prolixity and confusion of thought which pervade Reid's " Inquiry," of seventeen years' later

date.* Even Sir William Hamilton, learned historian and acute critic as he was, not only failed to apprehend the philosophical bearing of long-established physiological truths ; but, when he affirmed that there is no reason to deny that the mind feels at the finger points, and none to assert that the brain is the sole organ of thought, he showed that he had not apprehended the significance of the revolution commenced, two hundred years before his time, by Descartes, and effectively followed up by Haller, Hartley, and Bonnet, in the middle of the last century.†

In truth, the theory of sensation, except in one point, is, at the present moment, very much where Hartley, led by a hint of Sir Isaac Newton's, left it, when, a hundred and twenty years since, the "Observations on Man : his Frame, his Duty, and his Expectations," was laid before the world. The whole matter is put in a nutshell in the following passages of this notable book.

" External objects impressed upon the senses occasion, first on the nerves on which they are impressed, and then on the brain, vibrations' of the small and, as we may say, infinitesimal medullary particles.

" These vibrations are motions backward and forward of the small particles ; of the same kind with the oscillations of pendulums and the tremblings of the particles of sounding bodies. They must be conceived to be exceedingly short and small, so as not to have the least efficacy tc disturb or move the whole bodies of the nerves or brain." (Vol. 1, p. 11.)

---

* In justice to Reid, however, it should be stated that the chapters on sensation in the "Essays on the Intellectual Powers " (1785) exhibit a great improvement. He is, in fact, in advance of his commentator, as the note to Essay II. chap. ii. p. 248 of Hamilton's edition shows.

† Sir William Hamilton gravely informs his hearers:—" We have no more right to deny that the mind feels at the finger points, as consciousness assures us, than to assert that it thinks exclusively in the brain."— " Lecture on Metaphysics and Logic," ii. p. 128. " We have no reason whatever to doubt the report of consciousness, that we actually perceive at the external point of sensation, and that we perceive the material reality."—*Ibid.* p. 129.

"The white medullary substance of the brain is also the immediate instrument by which ideas are presented to the mind; or, in other words, whatever changes are made in this substance, corresponding changes are made in our ideas; and *vice versa.*" (*Ibid.* p. 8.)*

Hartley, like Haller, had no conception of the nature and functions of the gray matter of the brain. But, if for "white medullary substance," in the latter paragraph, we substitute "gray cellular substance," Hartley's propositions embody the most probable conclusions which are to be drawn from the latest investigations of physiologists. In order to judge how completely this is the case, it will be well to study some simple case of sensation, and, following the example of Reid and of James Mill, we may begin with the sense of smell. Suppose that I become aware of a musky scent, to which the name of "muskiness" may be given. I call this an odor, and I class it along with the feelings of light, colors, sounds, tastes, and the like, among those phenomena which are known as sensations. To say that I am aware of this phenomenon, or that I have it, or that it exists, are simply different modes of affirming the same facts. If I am asked how I know that it exists, I can only reply that its existence and my knowledge of it are one and the same thing; in short, that my knowledge is immediate or intuitive, and, as such, is possessed of the highest conceivable degree of certainty.

The pure sensation of muskiness is almost sure to be followed by a mental state which is not a sensation, but a belief, that there is somewhere close at hand a something on which the existence of the sensation depends. It may be a musk-deer, or a musk-rat, or a musk-plant, or a grain of dry musk, or simply a scented handker-

chief; but former experience leads us to believe that the sensation is due to the presence of one or other of these objects, and that it will vanish if the object is removed. In other words, there arises a belief in an external cause of the muskiness, which, in common language, is termed an odorous body.

But the manner in which this belief is usually put into words is strangely misleading. If we are dealing with a musk-plant, for example, we do not confine ourselves to a simple statement of that which we believe, and say that the musk-plant is the cause of the sensation called muskiness; but we say that the plant has a musky smell, and we speak of the odor as a quality, or property, inherent in the plant. And the inevitable reaction of words upon thought has in this case become so complete, and has penetrated so deeply, that when an accurate statement of the case—namely, that muskiness, inasmuch as the term denotes nothing but a sensation, is a mental state, and has no existence except as a mental phenomenon—is first brought under the notice of common-sense folks, it is usually regarded by them as what they are pleased to call a mere metaphysical paradox and a patent example of useless subtlety. Yet the slightest reflection must suffice to convince any one possessed of sound reasoning faculties, that it is as absurd to suppose that muskiness is a quality inherent in one plant, as it would be to imagine that pain is a quality inherent in another because we feel pain when a thorn pricks the finger.

Even the common-sense philosopher, *par excellence*, says of smell : " It appears to be a simple and original affection or feeling of the mind, altogether inexplicable and unaccountable. It is indeed impossible that it can be in anybody : it is a sensation, and a sensation can only be in a sentient thing." *

* The speculations of Bonnet are remarkably similar to those of Hartley; and they appear to have originated independently, though the " Essai de Psychologie " (1754) is of five years' later date than the " Observations on Man " (1749).

* "An Inquiry into the Human Mind on the Principles of Common Sense," chap. ii. § 2. Reid affirms that " it is genius, and not

That which is true of muskiness is true of every other odor. Lavender-smell, clove-smell, garlic-smell, are, like " muskiness," names of states of consciousness, and have no existence except as such. But, in ordinary language, we speak of all these odors as if they were independent entities residing in lavender, cloves, and garlic; and it is not without a certain struggle that the false metaphysic of so-called common sense, thus ingrained in us, is expelled.

For the present purpose, it is unnecessary to inquire into the origin of our belief in external bodies, or into that of the notion of causation. Assuming the existence of an external world, there is no difficulty in obtaining experimental proof that, as a general rule, olfactory sensations are caused by odorous bodies; and we may pass on to the next step of the inquiry—namely, how the odorous body produces the effect attributed to it.

The first point to be noted here is another fact revealed by experience; that the appearance of the sensation is governed, not only by the presence of the odorous substance, but by the condition of a certain part of our corporeal structure, the nose. If the nostrils are closed, the presence of the odorous substance does not give rise to the sensation ; while, when they are open, the sensation is intensified by the approximation of the odorous substance to them, and by snuffing up the adjacent air in such a manner as to draw it into the nose. On the other hand, looking at an odorous substance, or rubbing it on the skin, or holding it to the ear, does not awaken the sensation. Thus, it can be readily established by experiment that the perviousness of the nasal passages is, in some way, essential to the sensory function ; in fact, that the organ of that function is lodged somewhere in the nasal passages. And, since odorous bodies give rise to their effects at considerable distances, the suggestion is obvious that something must pass from them into the sense organ. What is this "something," which plays the part of an intermediary between the odorous body and the sensory organ ?

The oldest speculation about the matter dates back to Democritus and the Epicurean School, and it is to be found fully stated in the fourth book of Lucretius. It comes to this : that the surfaces of bodies are constantly throwing off excessively attenuated films of their own substance : and that these films, reaching the mind, excite the appropriate sensations in it.

Aristotle did not admit the existence of any such material films, but conceived that it was the form of the substance, and not its matter, which affected sense, as a seal impresses wax, without losing anything in the process. While many, if not the majority, of the Schoolmen took up an intermediate position and supposed that a something, which was not exactly either material or immaterial, and which they called an "intentional species," effected the needful communication between the bodily cause of sensation and the mind.

But all these notions, whatever may be said for or against them in general, are fundamentally defective, by reason of an oversight which was inevitable, in the state of knowledge at the time in which they were promulgated. What the older philosophers did not know, and could not know, before the anatomist and the physiologist had done their work, is that, between the external object and that mind in which they supposed the sensation to inhere, there lies a physical obstacle. The sense organ is not a mere passage by which the " tenuia simulacra rerum," or the "intentional

---

the want of it, that adulterates philosophy, and fills it with error and false theory ; " and no doubt his own lucubrations are free from the smallest taint of the impurity to which he objects. But, for want of something more than that sort of ". common sense," which is very common and a little dull, the contemner of genius did not notice that the admission here made knocks so big a hole in the bottom of " common sense philosophy," that nothing can save it from foundering in the dreaded abyss of Idealism.

species " cast off by objects, or the " forms " of sensible things, pass straight to the mind ; on the contrary, it stands as a firm and impervious barrier, through which no material particle of the world without can make its way to the world within.

Let us consider the olfactory sense organ more nearly. Each of the nostrils leads into a passage completely separated from the other by a partition, and these two passages place the nostrils in free communication with the back of the throat, so that they freely transmit the air passing to the lungs when the mouth is shut, as in ordinary breathing. The floor of each passage is flat, but its roof is a high arch, the crown of which is seated between the orbital cavities of the skull, which serve for the lodgment and protection of the eyes; and it therefore lies behind the apparent limits of that feature which, in ordinary language, is called the nose. From the side walls of the upper and back part of these arched chambers, certain delicate plates of bone project, and these, as well as a considerable part of the partition between the two chambers, are covered by a fine, soft, moist membrane. It is to this " Schneiderian," or olfactory, membrane that odorous bodies must obtain direct access, if they are to give rise to their appropriate sensations ; and it is upon the relatively large surface, which the olfactory membrane offers, that we must seek for the seat of the organ of the olfactory sense. The only essential part of that organ consists of a multitude of minute rodlike bodies, set perpendicularly to the surface of the membrane, and forming a part of the cellular coat, or epithelium, which covers the olfactory membrane, as the epidermis covers the skin. In the case of the olfactory sense, there can be no doubt that the Democritic hypothesis, at any rate for such odorous substances as musk, has a good foundation. Infinitesimal particles of musk fly off the surface of the odorous body, and, becoming diffused through the air, are carried into the nasal passages, and thence into the olfactory chambers, where they come into contact with the filamentous extremities of the delicate olfactory epithelium.

But this is not all. The "mind" is not, so to speak, upon the other side of the epithelium. On the contrary, the inner ends of the olfactory cells are connected with nerve fibers, and these nerve fibers, passing into the cavity of the skull, at length end in a part of the brain, the olfactory sensorium. It is certain that the integrity of each, and the physical inter-connection of all these three structures, the epithelium of the sensory organ, the nerve fibers, and the sensorium, are essential conditions of ordinary sensation. That is to say, the air in the olfactory chambers may be charged with particles of musk; but, if either the epithelium, or the nerve fibers, or the sensorium is injured, or if they are physically disconnected from one another, sensation will not arise. Moreover, the epithelium may be said to be receptive, the nerve fibers transmissive, and the sensorium sensifacient. For, in the act of smelling, the particles of the odorous substance produce a molecular change (which Hartley was in all probability right in terming a vibration) in the epithelium, and this change being transmitted to the nerve fibers, passes along them with a measurable velocity, and, finally reaching the sensorium, is immediately followed by the sensation.

Thus, modern investigation supplies a representative of the Epicurean simulacra in the volatile particles of the musk ; but it also gives us the stamp of the particles on the olfactory epithelium, without any transmission of matter, as the equivalent of the Aristotelian "form;" while, finally, the modes of motion of the molecules of the olfactory cells, of the nerve, and of the cerebral sensorium, which are Hartley's vibrations, may stand very well for a double of the "intentional species" of the Schoolmen. And this last remark is not intended merely to suggest a fanciful parallel; for, if the cause of the sensation is, as analogy suggests, to be sought in the mode of motion of the object of sense, then it is quite possible that the particular mode of motion of the object is reproduced in the sensorium; exactly as the diaphragm of a telephone reproduces the mode of motion taken up at its receiving end. In other words, the secondary "intentional species" may be, as the Schoolmen thought the primary one was, the last link between matter and mind.

None the less, however, does it remain true that no similarity exists, nor indeed is conceivable, between the cause of the sensation and the sensation. Attend as closely to the sensations of muskiness, or any other odor, as we will, no trace of extension, resistance, or motion is discernible in them. They have no attribute in common with those which we ascribe to matter; they are, in the strictest sense of the words, immaterial entities.

Thus, the most elementary study of sensation justifies Descartes' position, that we know more of mind than we do of body; that the immaterial world is a firmer reality than the material. For the sensation "muskiness" is known immediately. So long as it persists, it is a part of what we call our thinking selves, and its existence lies beyond the possibility of doubt. The knowledge of an objective or material cause of the sensation, on the other hand, is mediate; it is a belief as contradistinguished from an intuition; and it is a belief which, in any given instance of sensation, may by possibility, be devoid of foundation. For odors, like other sensations, may arise from the occurrence of the appropriate molecular changes in the nerve or in the sensorium, by the operation of a cause distinct from the affection of the sense organ by an odorous body. Such "subjective" sensations are as real existences as any others, and as distinctly suggest an external odorous object as their cause; but the belief thus generated is a delusion. And, if beliefs are properly termed "testimonies of consciousness," then undoubtedly the testimony of consciousness may be, and often is, untrustworthy.

Another very important consideration arises out of the facts as they are now known. That which, in the absence of a knowledge of the physiology of sensation, we call the cause of the smell, and term the odorous object, is only such, mediately, by reason of its emitting particles which give rise to a mode of motion in the sense organ. The sense organ, again, is only a mediate cause by reason of its producing a molecular change in the nerve fiber; while this last change is also only a mediate cause of sensation, depending, as it does, upon the change which it excites in the sensorium.

The sense organ, the nerve, and the sensorium, taken together, constitute the sensiferous apparatus. They make up the thickness of the wall between the mind, as represented by the sensation "muskiness" and the object, as represented by the particle of musk in contact with the olfactory epithelium.

It will be observed that the sensiferous wall and the external world are of the same nature; whatever it is that constitutes them both is expressible in terms of matter and motion. Whatever changes take place in the sensiferous apparatus are continuous with, and similar to, those which take place in the external world.* But with the sensorium, matter and motion come to an end; while phenomena of another order, or immaterial states of consciousness, make their appearance. How is the relation between the material and the immaterial phenomena to be conceived? This is the metaphysical problem of problems, and the solutions which have been suggested have been made the corner-stones of systems of philosophy. Three mutually

---

* See note on the next page.

irreconcilable readings of the riddle have been offered.

The first is, that an immaterial substance of mind exists; and that it is affected by the mode of motion of the sensorium in such a way as to give rise to the sensation

The second is, that the sensation is a direct effect of the mode of motion of the sensorium, brought about without the intervention of any substance of mind.

The third is, that the sensation is neither directly nor indirectly an effect of the mode of motion of the sensorium, but that it has an independent cause. Properly speaking, therefore, it is not an effect of the motion of the sensorium, but a concomitant of it.

As none of these hypotheses is capable of even an approximation to demonstration, it is almost needless to remark that they have been severally held with tenacity and advocated with passion. I do not think it can be said of any of the three that it is inconceivable, or that it can be assumed on *a priori* grounds to be impossible.

Consider the first, for example; an immaterial substance is perfectly conceivable. In fact, it is obvious that if we possessed no sensations but those of smell and hearing, we should be unable to conceive a material substance. We might have a conception of time, but could have none of extension, or of resistance or of motion. And without the three latter conceptions no idea of matter could be formed. Our whole knowledge would be limited to that of a shifting succession of immaterial phenomena. But, if an immaterial substance may exist, it may have any conceivable properties; and sensation may be one of them. All these propositions may be affirmed with complete dialectic safety, inasmuch as they cannot possibly be disproved; but neither can a particle of demonstrative evidence be offered in favor of the existence of an immaterial substance.

As regards the second hypothesis, it certainly is not inconceivable, and therefore it may be true, that sensation is the direct effect of certain kinds of bodily motion. It is just as easy to suppose this as to suppose, on the former hypothesis, that bodily motion affects an immaterial substance. But neither is it susceptible of proof.

And, as to the third hypothesis, since the logic of induction is in no case competent to prove that events apparently standing in the relation of

Note.—The following diagrammatic scheme may help to elucidate the theory of sensation:

	Mediate Knowledge			Immediate Knowledge.
	Sensiferous Apparatus			
Objects of Sense	Receptive (Sense Organ)	Transmissive (Nerve)	Sensificatory (Sensorium)	Sensations and other States of Consciousness
Hypothetical Substance of Matter.				Hypothetical Substance of Mind
	Physical World			Mental World
Not Self		Self		
	Non-Ego or Object			Ego or Subject

Immediate knowledge is confined to states of consciousness, or, in other words, to the phenomena of mind. Knowledge of the physical world, or of one's own body and of objects external to it, is a system of beliefs or judgments based on the sensations. The term "self" is applied not only to the series of mental phenomena which constitute the ego, but to the fragment of the physical world which is their constant concomitant. The corporeal self, therefore, is part of the non-ego; and is objective in relation to the ego as subject.

cause and effect may not both be effects of a common cause—that also is as safe from refutation, if as incapable of demonstration, as the other two.

In my own opinion, neither of these speculations can be regarded seriously as anything but a more or less convenient working hypothesis. But, if I must choose among them, I take the "law of parcimony" for my guide, and select the simplest—namely, that the sensation is the direct effect of the mode of motion of the sensorium. It may justly be said that this is not the slightest explanation of sensation ; but then am I really any the wiser, if I say that a sensation is an activity (of which I know nothing) of a substance of mind (of which also I know nothing)? Or, if I say that the Deity causes the sensation to arise in my mind immediately after He has caused the particles of the sensorium to move in a certain way, is anything gained ? In truth a sensation, as we have already seen, is an intuition—a part of immediate knowledge. As such, it is an ultimate fact and inexplicable ; and all that we can hope to find out about it, and that indeed is worth finding out, is its relation to other natural facts. That relation appears to me to be sufficiently expressed, for all practical purposes, by saying that sensation is the invariable consequent of certain changes in the sensorium— or, in other words, that, so far as we know, the change in the sensorium is the cause of the sensation.

I permit myself to imagine that the untutored, if noble, savage of "common sense" who has been misled into reading thus far by the hope of getting positive solid information about sensation, giving way to not unnatural irritation, may here interpellate : "The upshot of all this long disquisition is that we are profoundly ignorant. We knew that to begin with, and you have merely furnished another example of the emptiness and uselessness of metaphysics." But I venture to reply, Pardon me, you were ignorant, but you did not know it.

On the contrary, you thought you knew a great deal, and were quite satisfied with the particularly absurd metaphysical notions which you were pleased to call the teachings of common sense. You thought that your sensations were properties of external things, and had an existence outside of yourself. You thought that you knew more about material than you do about immaterial existences. And if, as a wise man has assured us, the knowledge of what we don't know is the next best thing to the knowledge of what we do know, this brief excursion into the province of philosophy has been highly profitable. Of all the dangerous mental habits, that which schoolboys call "cocksureness" is probably the most perilous ; and the inestimable value of metaphysical discipline is that it furnishes an effectual counterpoise to this evil proclivity. Whoso has mastered the elements of philosophy knows that the attribute of unquestionable certainty appertains only to the existence of a state of consciousness so long as it exists ; all other beliefs are mere probabilities of a higher or lower order. Sound metaphysic is an amulet which renders its professor proof alike against the poison of superstition and the counterpoison of nihilism ; by showing that the affirmations of the former and the denials of the latter alike deal with matters about which, for lack of evidence, nothing can be either affirmed or denied.

I have dwelt at length upon the nature and origin of our sensations of smell, on account of the comparative freedom of the olfactory sense from the complications which are met with in most of the other senses. Sensations of taste, however, are generated in almost as simple a fashion as those of smell. In this case, the sense organ is the epithelium which covers the tongue and the palate · and which sometimes, becoming modified, gives rise to peculiar organs termed "gustatory bulbs," in which the epithelial cells elongate and assume a somewhat rod-like form. Nerve fibers connect the sensory organ with the sensorium, and tastes or flavors are states of consciousness caused by the change of molecular state of the latter. In the case of the sense of touch there is often no sense organ distinct from the general epidermis. But many fishes and amphibia exhibit local modifications of the epidermic cells which are sometimes extraordinarily like the gustatory bulbs; more commonly, both in lower and higher animals, the effect of the contact of external bodies is intensified by the development of hairlike filaments, or of true hairs, the bases of which are in immediate relation with the ends of the sensory nerves. Every one must have noticed the extreme delicacy of the sensations produced by the contact of bodies with the ends of the hairs of the head; and the "whiskers" of cats owe their functional importance to the abundant supply of nerves to the follicles in which their bases are lodged. What part, if any, the so-called "tactile corpuscles," "end bulbs," and "Pacinian bodies," play in the mechanism of touch is unknown. If they are sense organs, they are exceptional in character, in so far as they do not appear to be modifications of the epidermis. Nothing is known respecting the organs of those sensations of resistance which are grouped under the head of the muscular sense; nor of the sensations of warmth and cold; nor of that very singular sensation which we call tickling.

In the case of heat and cold, the organism not only becomes affected by external bodies, far more remote than those which affect the sense of smell; but the Democritic hypothesis is obviously no longer permissible. When the direct rays of the sun fall upon the skin, the sensation of heat is certainly not caused by "attenuated films" thrown off from that luminary, but is due to a mode of motion which is transmitted to us In

Aristotelian phrase, it is the form without the matter of the sun which stamps the sense organ; and this, translated into modern language, means nearly the same thing as Hartley's vibrations. Thus we are prepared for what happens in the case of the auditory and the visual senses. For neither the ear, nor the eye, receives anything but the impulses or vibrations originated by sonorous or luminous bodies. Nevertheless, the receptive apparatus still consists of nothing but specially modified epithelial cells. In the labyrinth of the ear of the higher animals, the free ends of these cells terminate in excessively delicate hair-like filaments; while, in the lower forms of auditory organ, its free surface is beset with delicate hairs like those of the surface of the body, and the transmissive nerves are connected with the bases of these hairs. Thus there is an insensible gradation in the forms of the receptive apparatus from the organ of touch, on the one hand, to those of taste and smell; and, on the other hand, to that of hearing. Even in the case of the most refined of all the sense organs, that of vision, the receptive apparatus departs but little from the general type. The only essential constituent of the visual sense organ is the retina, which forms so small a part of the eyes of the higher animals; and the simplest eyes are nothing but portions of the integument, in which the cells of the epidermis have become converted into glassy, rod-like retinal corpuscles. The outer ends of these are turned toward the light; their sides are more or less extensively coated with a dark pigment, and their inner ends are connected with the transmissive nerve fibers. The light, impinging on these visual rods, produces a change in them which is communicated to the nerve fibers, and, being transmitted to the sensorium, gives rise to the sensation—if indeed all animals which possess eyes are endowed with what we understand as sensation.

In the higher animals, a complicated appartus of lenses, arranged on the principle of a camera obscura, serves at once to concentrate and to individualize the pencils of light proceeding from external bodies. But the essential part of the organ of vision is still a layer of cells, which have the form of rods with truncated or conical ends. By what seems a strange anomaly, however, the glassy ends of these are turned not toward, but away from, the light; and the latter has to traverse the layer of nervous tissues with which their outer ends are connected, before it can affect them. Moreover, the rods and cones of the vertebrate retina are so deeply seated, and in many respects so peculiar in character, that it appears impossible, at first sight, that they can have any thing to do with that epidermis of which gustatory and tactile, and at any rate the lower forms of auditory and visual, organs are obvious modifications.

Whatever be the apparent diversities among the sensiferous apparatuses, however, they share certain common characters. Each consists of a receptive, a transmissive, and a sensificatory portion. The essential part of the first is an epithelium, of the second, nerve fibers, of the third, a part of the brain; the sensation is always the consequence of the mode of motion excited in the receptive, and sent along the transmissive, to the sensificatory part of the sensiferous apparatus. And, in all the senses, there is no likeness whatever between the object of sense, which is matter in motion, and the sensation, which is an immaterial phenomena.

On the hypothesis which appears to me to be the most convenient, sensation is a product of the sensiferous apparatus caused by certain modes of motion which are set up in it by impulses from without. The sensiferous apparatuses are, as it were, factories, all of which at the one end receive raw materials of a similar kind—namely, modes of motion—while, at the other, each turns out a special product, the feeling which constitutes the kind of sensation characteristic of it.

Or, to make use of a closer comparison, each sensiferous apparatus is comparable to a musical-box wound up; with as many tunes as there are separate sensations. The object of a simple sensation is the agent which presses down the stop of one of these tunes, and the more feeble the agent, the more delicate must be the mobility of the stop.

But if this be true, if the recipient part of the sensiferous apparatus is, in all cases, merely a mechanism affected by coarser or finer kinds of material motion, we might expect to find that all sense organs are fundamentally alike, and result from the modification of the same morphological elements. And this is exactly what does result from all recent histological and embryological investigations.

It has been seen that the receptive part of the olfactory apparatus is a slightly modified epithelium, which lines an olfactory chamber deeply seated between the orbits in adult human beings. But, if we trace back the nasal chambers to their origin in the embryo, we find, that, to begin with, they are mere depressions of the skin of the fore part of the head, lined by a continuation of the general epidermis. These depressions become pits, and the pits, by the growth of the adjacent parts, gradually acquire the position which they finally occupy. The olfactory organ, therefore, is a specially modified part of the general integument.

The human ear would seem to present greater difficulties. For the essential part of the sense organ, in this case, is the membranous labyrinth, a bag of complicated form, which lies buried in the depths of the floor of the skull, and is surrounded by dense and solid bone. Here, however, recourse to the study of development readily unravels the mystery. Shortly after the time when the olfactory organ appears, as a depression of the skin on the side of the fore part of the head, the auditory organ appears, as a similar depression on the side of its back part. The depression, rapidly deepening, becomes a small pouch ; and then, the communication with the exterior becoming shut off, the pouch is converted into a closed bag, the epithelial lining of which is a part of the general epidermis segregated from the rest. The adjacent tissues, changing first into cartilage and then into bone, enclose the auditory sac in a strong case, in which it undergoes its further metamorphoses ; while the drum, the ear bones, and the external ear, are superadded by no less extraordinary modifications of the adjacent parts. Still more marvelous is the history of the development of the organ of vision. In the place of the eye, as in that of the nose and that of the ear, the young embryo presents a depression of the general integument ; but, in man and the higher animals, this does not give rise to the proper sensory organ, but only to part of the accessory structures concerned in vision. In fact, this depression, deepening and becoming converted into a shut sac, produces only the cornea, the aqueous humor, and the crystalline lens of the perfect eye.

The retina is added to this by the outgrowth of the wall of a portion of the brain into a sort of bag, or sac, with a narrow neck, the convex bottom of which is turned outward, or toward the crystalline lens. As the development of the eye proceeds, the convex bottom of the bag becomes pushed in, so that it gradually obliterates the cavity of the sac, the previously convex wall of which becomes deeply concave. The sac of the brain is now like a double nightcap ready for the head, but the place which the head would occupy is taken by the vitreous humor, while the layer of nightcap next it becomes the retina. The cells of this layer which lie farthest from the vitreous humor, or, in other words, bound the original cavity of the sac, are metamorphosed into the rods and cones. Suppose now that the sac of the brain could be brought back to its original form ; then the rods and cones would form part of the lining of a side pouch of the brain. But one of the most wonderful revelations of embryology is the proof of the fact that the brain itself is, at its first beginning, merely an infolding of the epidermic layer of the general integument. Hence it follows that the rods and cones of the vertebrate eye are modified epidermic cells, as much as the crystalline cones of the insect or crustacean eye are ; and that the inversion of the position of the former in relation to light arises simply from the roundabout way in which the vertebrate retina is developed.

Thus all the higher sense organs start from one foundation, and the receptive epithelium of the eye, or of the ear, is as much modified epidermis as is that of the nose. The structural unity of the sense organs is the morphological parallel to their identity of physiological function, which, as we have seen, is to be impressed by certain modes of motion ; and they are fine or coarse, in proportion to the delicacy or the strength of the impulses by which they are to be affected.

In ultimate analysis, then, it appears that a sensation is the equivalent in terms of consciousness for a mode of motion of the matter of the sensorium. But, if inquiry is pushed a stage farther, and the question is asked, What then do we know about matter and motion ? there is but one reply possible. All that we know about motion is that it is a name for certain changes in the relations of our visual, tactile, and muscular sensations ; and all that we know about matter is that it is the hypothetical substance of physical phenomena—the assumption of the existence of which is as pure a piece of metaphysical speculation as is that of the existence of the substance of mind.

Our sensations, our pleasures, our pains, and the relations of these, make up the sum total of the elements of positive, unquestionable knowledge. We call a large section of these sensations and their relations matter and motion; the rest we term mind and thinking; and experience shows that there is a certain constant order of succession between some of the former and some of the latter.

This is all that just metaphysical criticism leaves of the idols set up by the spurious metaphysics of vulgar common sense. It is consistent either with pure Materialism, or with pure Idealism, but it is neither. For the Idealist, not content with declaring the truth that our knowledge is limited to facts of consciousness, affirms the wholly unprovable proposition that nothing exists beyond these and the substance of mind. And, on the other hand, the Materialist, holding by the truth that, for anything that appears to the contrary, material phenomena are the causes of mental phenomena, asserts his unprovable dogma, that material phenomena and the substance of matter are the sole primary existences.

Strike out the propositions about which neither controversialist does or can know anything, and there is nothing left for them to quarrel about. Make a desert of the Unknowable, and the divine Astræa of philosophic peace will commence her blessed reign.

———

V.

ON CERTAIN ERRORS RESPECTING THE STRUCTURE OF THE HEART ATTRIBUTED TO ARISTOTLE.

IN all the commentaries upon the "Historia Animalium" which I have met with, Aristotle's express and repeated statement, that the heart of man and the largest animals contains only three cavities, is noted as a remarkable error. Even Cuvier, who had a great advantage over most of the commentators in his familiarity with the subject of Aristotle's descrip-

tion, and whose habitual caution and moderation seem to desert him when the opportunity of panegyrizing the philosopher presents itself, is betrayed into something like a sneer on this topic. "He gives to that organ only three cavities—an error which at least shows that he had observed its structure." ("Histoire des Sciences Naturelles," i. p. 152.)

To which remark, what follows will, I think, justify the reply, that it "at least shows" that Cuvier had not given ordinary attention, to say nothing of the careful study which they deserve, to sundry passages in the first and the third books of the "Historia" which I proceed to lay before the reader.

For convenience of reference these passages are marked *A*, *B*, *C*, etc.*

Book i. 17.—(*A*) "The heart has three cavities, it lies above the lung on the division of the windpipe, and has a fatty and thick membrane where it is united with the great vein and the aorta. It lies upon the aorta, with its point down the chest, in all animals that have a chest. In all, alike in those that have a chest and in those that have none, the foremost part of it is the apex. This is often overlooked through the turning upside down of the dissection. The rounded end of the heart is uppermost, the pointed end of it is largely fleshy and thick, and in its cavities there are tendons. In other animals which have a chest the heart lies in the middle of the chest; in men, more to the left side, between the nipples, a little inclined to the left nipple in the upper part of the chest. The heart is not large, and its general form is not elongated but rounded, except that the apex is produced into a point.

(*B*) "It has, as already stated, three cavities, the largest of them is on the right, the smallest on the left, the middle-sized one in the middle; they have all, also the two small ones, passages (τετρημένας) toward the lung, very evidently as respects one of the cavities. In the region of the union [with the great vein and the aorta] the largest cavity is connected with the largest vein (near which is the mesentery); the middle cavity with the aorta.

———

* The text I have followed is that given by Aubert and Wimmer, "Aristoteles Thierkunde: kritisch berichtigter Text mit deutschen Uebersetzung;" but I have tried here and there to bring the English version rather closer to the original than the German translation, excellent as it is, seems to me to be.

(C) " Canals (πόροι) from the heart pass to the lung and divide in the same fashion as the windpipe does, closely accompanying those from the windpipe through the whole lung. The canals from the heart are uppermost.

(D) " No canal is common [to the branches of the windpipe and those of the vein] but through those parts of them which are in contact, the air passes in and they [the πόροι] carry it to the heart.

(E) " One of the canals leads to the right cavity, the other to the left.

(F) " Of all the viscera, the heart alone contains blood [in itself]. The lung contains blood, not in itself but in the veins, the heart in itself; for in each of the cavities there is blood; the thinnest is in the middle cavity.

Book iii. 3.—(G) " Two veins lie in the thorax alongside the spine, on its inner face; the larger more forward, the smaller behind; the larger more to the right, the smaller, which some call *aorta* (on account of the tendinous part of it seen in dead bodies), to the left. These take their origin from the heart; they pass entire, preserving the nature of veins, through the other viscera that they reach; while the heart is rather a part of them, and more especially of the anterior and larger one, which is continued into veins above and below, while between these is the heart.

(H) " All hearts contain cavities, but in those of very small animals, the largest [cavity] is hardly visible, those of middling size have another, and the biggest all three.

(I) " The point of the heart is directed forward, as was mentioned at first; the largest cavity to the right and upper side of it, the smallest to the left, and the middle-sized one between these; both of these are much smaller than the largest.

(K) " They are all connected by passages (συντέτρηνται) with the lung, but, on account of the smallness of the canals, this is obscure except in one.

(L) " The great vein proceeds from the largest cavity which lies upward and to the right; next through the hollow middle part it becomes vein again, this cavity being a part of the vein in which the blood stagnates.

(M) " The aorta [proceeds from] the middle [cavity], but not in the same way, for it is connected [with the middle cavity] by a much more narrow tube.

(N) " The [great] vein extends through the heart, toward the aorta from the heart.

(O) " The great vein is membranous like skin, the aorta narrower than it and very tendinous, and as it extends toward the head and the lower parts it becomes narrow and altogether tendinous.

(P) " In the first place, a part of the great vein extends upward from the heart toward the lung and the attachment of the aorta, the vein being large and undivided. It divides into two parts, the one to the lung, the other to the spine and the lowest vertebra of the neck.

(Q) " The vein which extends to the lung first divides into two parts for the two halves of it and then extends alongside each tube, and each passage, the larger beside the larger and the smaller beside the smaller, so that no part [of the lung] can be found from which a passage, and a vein are absent. The terminations are invisible on account of their minuteness, but the whole lung appears full of blood. The canals from the vein lie above the tubes given off from the windpipe."

The key to the whole of the foregoing description of the heart lies in the passages (G) and (L). They prove that Aristotle, like Galen, five hundred years afterward, and like the great majority of the old Greek anatomists, did not reckon what we call the right auricle as a constituent of the heart at all, but as a hollow part, or dilatation, of the " great vein." Aristotle is careful to state that his observations were conducted on suffocated animals; and if any one will lay open the thorax of a dog or a rabbit, which has been killed with chloroform, in such a manner as to avoid wounding any important vessel, he will at once see why Aristotle adopted this view.

For, as the subjoined figure (p. 45) shows, the vena cava inferior (*b*), the right auricle (*R.a.*) and the vena cava superior and innominate vein (*V.I.*) distended with blood seem to form one continuous column, to which the heart is attached as a sort of appendage. This column is, as Aristotle says, vein above (*a*) and vein below (*b*), the upper and the lower divisions being connected by means of the intervening cavity or chamber (*R.a.*)—which is that which we call the right auricle.

But when, from the four cavities of the heart recognized by us moderns, one is excluded, there remain three—which is just what Aristotle says. The solution of the difficulty is, in fact, as absurdly simple as that presented by the egg of Columbus; and any error there may be, is not to be put down to Aristotle, but to that inability to comprehend that the same fact may be accurately described in different ways, which is the special characteristic of the commentatorial mind. That the three cavities mentioned by Aristotle are just those which remain if the right auricle is omitted, is plain enough from what is said in (*B*), (*C*), (*E*), (*I*), and (*L*). For, in a suffocated animal, the "right cavity" which is directly connected with the great vein, and is obviously the right ventricle, being distended with blood, will look much larger than the middle cavity, which, since it gives rise to the aorta, can only be the left ventricle. And this, again, will appear larger than the thin and collapsed left auricle, which must be Aristotle's left cavity, inasmuch as this cavity is said to be connected by πόροι with the lung. The reason why Aristotle considered the left auricle to be a part of the heart, while he merged the right auricle in the great vein, is, obviously, the small relative size of the venous trunks and their sharper demarkation from the auricle. Galen, however, perhaps more consistently, regarded the left auricle also as a

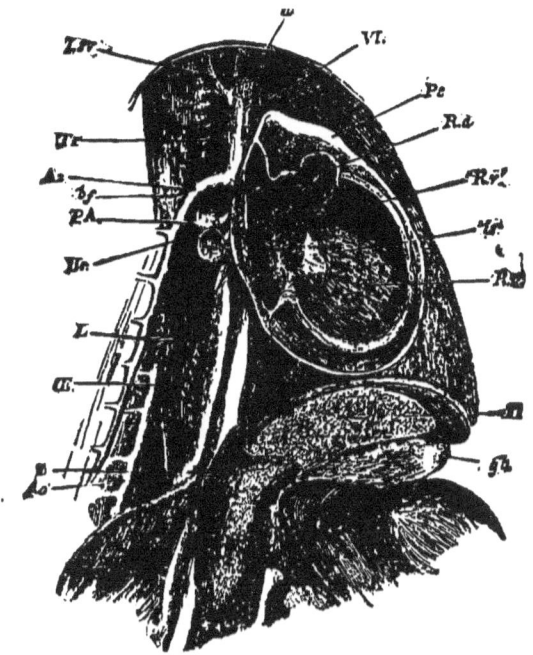

A dog having been killed by chloroform, enough of the right wall of the thorax was removed, without any notable bleeding, to expose the thoracic viscera. A carefully measured outline sketch of the parts *in situ* was then made, and on dissection, twenty-four hours afterward, the necessary anatomical details were added. The woodcut is a faithfully reduced copy of the drawing thus constructed; and it represents the relations of the heart and great vessels as Aristotle saw them in a suffocated animal.

All but the inner lobe of the right lung has been removed; as well as the right half of the pericardium and the right walls of the right auricle and ventricle. It must be remembered that the thin transparent pericardial membrane appears nothing like so distinct in nature.

v.b., Aristotle's "great vein"; *V.I.*, right vena innominata and vena cava superior; *b*, the inferior vena cava; *R.a.*, the "hollow middle" part of the great vein or the right auricle ; *R.v'*, the prolongation of the cavity of the right ventricle *R.v* towards the pulmonary artery; *tr*, one of the tricuspid valves; *Pc*, the pericardium; *I.sv*, superior intercostal vein; *Az*, vena azygos; *P.A.*, right pulmonary artery; *Br*, right bronchus; *L*, inner lobe of the right lung; *Œ*, œsophagus; *Ao*, descending aorta; *H*, liver, in section, with hepatic vein, vena portæ, and gall-bladder, *gb*, separated by the diaphragm, also seen in section, from the thoracic cavity.

mere part of the "arteria venosa." The canal which leads from the right cavity of the heart to the lung (or, as Aristotle puts it (*E*), from the lung to the heart) is, without doubt, the pulmonary artery. But it may be said that, in this case, Aristotle contradicts himself, inasmuch as in (*P*) and (*Q*) a vessel, which is obviously the pulmonary artery, is described as a branch of the great vein. However, this difficulty also disappears, if we reflect that, in Aristotle's way of looking at the matter, the line of demarkation between the great vein and the heart coincides with the right auriculoventricular aperture; and that, inasmuch as the conical prolongation of the right ventricle which leads to the pulmonary artery (*R.v′* in the Figure), lies close in front of the auricle, its base may very easily (as the figure shows) be regarded as a part of the general opening of the great vein into the right ventricle. In fact, it is clear that Aristotle, having failed to notice the valves of the heart, did not distinguish the part of the right ventricle from which the pulmonary artery arises (*R.v′*) from the proper trunk of the artery on the one hand, and from the right auricle (*R.a.*) on the other. Thus the root, as we may call it, of the pulmonary artery and the right auricle, taken together, are spoken of as the " part of the great vein which extends upward "(*P*); and, as the vena-azygos (*Az*) was one branch of this, so the " vein to the lung " was regarded as another branch of it. But the latter branch, being given off close to the connection of the great vein with the ventricle, was also counted as one of the two πόροι by which the " heart " (that is to say the right ventricle, the left ventricle, and the left auricle of our nomenclature) communicates with the lung.

The only other difficulty that I observe is connected with (*K*). If Aristotle intended by this to affirm that the middle cavity (the left ventricle), like the other two, is directly connected with the lung by a πόρος, he would be in error. But he has ex-

cluded this interpretation of his words by (*E*), in which the number and relations of the canals, the existence of which he admits, are distinctly defined. I can only imagine then, that, so far as this passage applies to the left ventricle, it merely refers to the indirect communication of that cavity with the vessels of the lungs, through the left auricle.

On this evidence I submit that there is no escape from the conclusion that, instead of having committed a gross blunder, Aristotle has given a description of the heart which, so far as it goes, is remarkably accurate. He is in error only in regard to the differences which he imagines to exist between large and small hearts (*H*).

Cuvier (who has been followed by other commentators) ascribes another error to Aristotle :—" Aristotle supposed that the trachea, the windpipe, is prolonged to the heart, and seems to believe in consequence that the air penetrates thither " (l. c. p. 152).

Upon what foundation Cuvier rested the first of these two assertions, I am at a loss to divine. As a matter of fact, it will appear from the following excerpts that Aristotle gives an account of the structure of the lungs which is almost as good as that of the heart, and that it contains nothing about any prolongation of the windpipe to the heart.

" Within the neck lie what is called the œsophagus (so named on account of its length and its narrowness) and the windpipe. The position of the windpipe in all animals that have one, is in front of the œsophagus. All animals which possess a lung have a windpipe. The windpipe is of a cartilaginous nature and is exsanguine but is surrounded by many little veins. . . .

" It goes downward toward the middle of the lung, and then divides for each of the halves of the lung. In all animals that possess one, the lung is divided into two parts ; but, in those which bring forth their young alive, the separation is not equally well marked, least of all in man.

" In oviparous animals, such as birds, and in quadrupeds which are oviparous, the one half of the lung is widely separated from the other ; so that it appears as if they had two lungs. And from being single, the windpipe becomes (divided into) two, which extend to each half of the lung. It is fastened to the great vein, and to what is called the aorta. When the windpipe is blown up, the air passes into the hollow parts of the lung. In these, are cartilaginous tubes ($\delta\iota\alpha\phi\acute{v}\sigma\epsilon\iota\varsigma$) which unite at an angle; from the tubes passages ($\tau\rho\acute{\eta}\mu\alpha\tau\alpha$) traverse the whole of the lung; they are continually given off, the smaller from the larger." (Book i. 16.)

That Aristotle should speak of the lung as a single organ divided into two halves, and should say that the division is least marked in man, is puzzling at first; but the statement becomes intelligible, if we reflect upon the close union of the bronchi, the pulmonary vessels and the mediastinal walls of the pleuræ, in mammals; * and it is quite true that the lungs are much more obviously distinct from one another in birds.

Aubert and Wimmer translate the last paragraph of the passage just cited as follows:—

"Diese haben aber knorpelige Scheidewände, welche unter spitzen Winkeln zusammentreten, und aus ihnen führen Oeffnungen durch die ganze Lunge, indem sie sich in immer kleineren verzweigen."

But I cannot think that by $\delta\iota\alpha\phi\acute{v}\sigma\epsilon\iota\varsigma$ and $\tau\rho\acute{\eta}\mu\alpha\tau\alpha$, in this passage, Aristotle meant either "partitions" or openings in the ordinary sense of the latter word. For, in Book iii. Cap. 3, in describing the distribution of the "vein which goes to the lung" (the pulmonary artery), he says that it

"extends alongside each tube ($\sigma\acute{v}\rho\iota\gamma\gamma\alpha$) and each passage ($\tau\rho\hat{\eta}\mu\alpha$), the larger beside the larger, and the smaller beside the smaller; so that no part (of the lung) can be found from which a passage ($\tau\rho\hat{\eta}\mu\alpha$) and a vein are absent."

Moreover, in Book i. 17, he says—

"Canals ($\pi\acute{o}\rho o\iota$) from the heart pass to the lung and divide in the same fashion as the windpipe does, closely accompanying those from the windpipe through the whole lung."

And again in Book i. 17—

"It (the lung) is entirely spongy, and a long-

* In modern works on Veterinary Anatomy the lungs are sometimes described as two lobes of a single organ.

side of each tube ($\sigma\acute{v}\rho\iota\gamma\gamma\alpha$) run canals ($\pi\acute{o}\rho o\iota$) from the great vein."

On comparing the last three statements with the facts of the case, it is plain that by $\sigma\acute{v}\rho\iota\gamma\gamma\epsilon\varsigma$, or tubes, Aristotle means the bronchi and so many of their larger divisions as obviously contain cartilages; and that by $\delta\iota\alpha\phi\acute{v}\sigma\epsilon\iota\varsigma$ $\chi o\nu\delta\rho\acute{\omega}\delta\epsilon\iota\varsigma$ he denotes the same things; and, if this be so, then the $\tau\rho\acute{\eta}\mu\alpha\tau\alpha$ must be the smaller bronchial canals, in which the cartilages disappear.

This view of the structure of the lung [is perfectly correct so far as it extends; and, bearing it in mind, we shall be in a position to understand what Aristotle thought about the passage of air from the lungs into the heart. In every part of the lung, he says, in effect, there is an air tube which is derived from the trachea, and other tubes which are derived from the $\pi\acute{o}\rho o\iota$ which connect the lung with the heart (*suprà, C*). Their applied walls constitute the thin "synapses" ($\tau\grave{\eta}\nu$ $\sigma\acute{v}\nu\alpha\psi\iota\nu$) through which the air passes out of the air tubes into the $\pi\acute{o}\rho o\iota$, or blood vessels, by transudation or diffusion; for there is no community between the cavities of the air tubes and cavities of the canals; that is to say, no opening from one into the other (*suprà, D*).

On the words "$\kappa o\iota\nu\grave{o}\varsigma$ $\pi\acute{o}\rho o\varsigma$" Aubert and Wimmer remark (*l. c.* p. 239), "Da A. die Ansicht hat die Lungenluft würde dem Herzen zugeführt, so postulirt er statt vieler kleiner Verbindungen einen grossen Verbindungsgang zwischen Lunge und Herz."

But does Aristotle make this assumption? The only evidence so far as I know in favor of the affirmative answer to this question is the following passage:—

"The heart and the windpipe are connected by fatty and cartilaginous and fibrous bands; where they are connected it is hollow. Blowing into the windpipe does not show clearly in some animals, but in the larger animals it is clear that the air goes into it." (i. cap. 16.)

Aubert and Wimmer give a somewhat different rendering of this passage :—

"Auch das Herz hängt mit der Luftröhre durch fettreiche, knorpelige und faserige Bänder zusammen; und da, wo sie zusammenhängen, ist eine Höhlung. Beim Aufblasen der Lunge wird es bei manchen Thieren nicht wahrnehmbar, bei den grösseren aber ist es offenbar, dass die Luft in das Herz gelangt."

The sense here turns upon the signification which is to be ascribed to *into it* (εἰς αὐτὴν). But if these words refer to the heart, then Aristotle has distinctly pointed out the road which the air, in his opinion, takes, namely, through the "synapses" (*D*); and there is no reason that I can discover to believe that he "postulated" any other and more direct communication. With respect to the meaning of κοῖλόν ἐστιν (*it is hollow*), Aubert and Wimmer observe :—

"Dies scheint wohl die kurze Lungenvene zu sein. Schneider bezieht dies auf die Vorkammern, allein diese werden unten als Höhlen des Herzens beschrieben."

I am disposed to think, on the contrary, that the words refer simply to the cavity of the pericardium. For a part of this cavity (*sinus transversus pericardii*) lies between the aorta, on the one hand, and the pulmonary vessels with the bifurcation of the trachea, on the other hand, and is much more conspicuous in some animals than in man. It is strictly correct, therefore, in Aristotle's words, to say that where the heart and the windpipe are connected "it is hollow." If he had meant to speak of one of the pulmonary veins, or of any of the cavities of the heart, he would have used the terms πόροι or κοιλίας which he always employs for these parts.

According to Aristotle, then, the air taken into the lungs passes, from the final ramifications of the bronchial tubes into the corresponding branches of the pulmonary blood-vessels, not through openings, but by transudation, or, as we should nowadays say, diffusion, through the thin partitions formed by the applied coats of the two sets of canals. But the "pneuma" which thus reached the interior of the blood-vessels was not, in Aristotle's opinion, exactly the same thing as the air. It was "ἀὴρ πολὺς ῥέων καὶ ἀθρόος" ("De Mundo," iv. 9)—subtilized and condensed air; and it is hard to make out whether Aristotle considered it to possess the physical properties of an elastic fluid or those of a liquid. As he affirms that all the cavities of the heart contain blood (*F*), it is clear that he did not hold the erroneous view propounded in the next generation by Erasistratus. On the other hand, the fact that he supposes that the spermatic arteries do not contain blood but only an αἱματῶδης ὑγρόν ("Hist. Animalium," iii. 1), shows that his notions respecting the contents of the arteries were vague. Nor does he seem to have known that the pulse is characteristic only of the arteries; and as he thought that the arteries end in solid fibrous bands, he naturally could not have entertained the faintest conception of the true motion of the blood. But, without attempting to read into Aristotle modern conceptions which never entered his mind, it is only just to observe that his view of what becomes of the air taken into the lungs is by no means worthy of contempt as a gross error. On the contrary, here, as in the case of his anatomy of the heart, what Aristotle asserts is true as far as it goes. Something does actually pass from the air contained in the lungs through the coats of the vessels into the blood, and thence to the heart; to wit, oxygen. And I think that it speaks very well for ancient Greek science that the investigator of so difficult a physiological problem as that of respiration, should have arrived at a conclusion, the statement of which, after the lapse of more than two thousand years, can be accepted as a thoroughly established scientific truth.

I trust that the case in favor of removing the statements about the heart, from the list of the "errors of

Aristotle " is now clear ; and that the evidence proves, on the contrary, that they justify us in forming a very favorable estimate of the oldest anatomical investigations among the Greeks of which any sufficient record remains.

But is Aristotle to be credited· with the merit of having ascertained so much of the truth? This question will not appear superfluous to those who are acquainted with the extraordinary history of Aristotle's works, or who adopt the conclusion of Aubert and Wimmer, that, of the ten books of the "Historia Animalium" which have come down to us, three are largely or entirely spurious, and that the others contain many interpolations by later writers.

It so happens, however, that, apart from other reasons, there are satisfactory internal grounds for ascribing the account of the heart to a writer of the time at which Aristotle lived.

For, within thirty years of his death, the anatomists of the Alexandrian school had thoroughly investigated the structure and the functions of the valves of the heart. During this time the manuscripts of Aristotle were in the possession of Theophrastus ; and no interpolator of later date would have shown that he was ignorant of the nature and significance of these important structures, by the brief and obscure allusion—"in its cavities there are tendons " (A). On the other hand, Polybus, whose account of the vascular system is quoted in the "Historia Animalium," was an elder contemporary of Aristotle. Hence, if any part of the work faithfully represents that which Aristotle taught, we may safely conclude that the description of the heart does so. Having granted this much, however, it is another question, whether Aristotle is to be regarded as the first discoverer of the facts which he has so well stated, or whether he, like other men, was the intellectual child of his time and simply carried on a step or two the work which had been commenced by others.

On the subject of Aristotle's signifi-cance as an original worker in biology extraordinarily divergent views have been put forward. If we are to adopt Cuvier's estimate, Aristotle was simply a miracle :—

" Before Aristotle, philosophy, being entirely speculative, lost itself in baseless abstractions : science did not exist. Science would seem to have sprung completely forward from the brain of Aristotle, as Minerva sprung fully armed from the brain of Jupiter. Indeed this one man, without predecessors, without borrowing aught from the ages that went before, as they had produced nothing of solid merit, discovered and demonstrated a greater number of truths, performed more scientific work in a lifetime of 62 years than 20 centuries have been able to perform since," etc. "Aristotle was the first to introduce the method of induction, comparison and observation, in order to reach general ideas, and the method of experiment in order to multiply the facts from which these general ideas may be deduced." ("Hist. des Sciences Nat." t. i. p. 130 ; t. ii. p. 515.)

The late Mr. G. H. Lewes, on the contrary, tells us " on a superficial examination, therefore, he [Aristotle] will seem to have given tolerable descriptions ; especially if approached with that disposition to discover marvels which unconsciously determines us in our study of eminent writers. But a more unbiased and impartial criticism will disclose that he has given no single anatomical description of the least value. All that he knew may have been known, and probably was known, without dissection. . . . I do not assert that he never opened an animal ; on the contrary it seems highly probable that he had opened many. . . . He never followed the course of a vessel or a nerve ; never laid bare the origin and insertion of a muscle ; never discriminated the component parts of organs ; never made clear to himself the connection of organs into systems."—("Aristotle, a Chapter from the History of Science," pp. 156–7.)

In the face of the description of the heart and lungs, just quoted, I think we may venture to say that no one who has acquired even an elementary practical acquaintance with anatomy, and knows of his own knowledge that which Aristotle describes, will agree with the opinion expressed by Mr. Lewes ; and those who turn to the accounts of the structure of the rock lobster and the common lobster, or to that of the Cephalopods and other Mollusks, in the fourth book of the "Historia Animalium," will probably feel inclined to object to it still more strongly.

On the other hand, Cuvier's exaggerated panegyric will as little bear the test of cool discussion. In Greece, the century before Aristotle's birth was a period of great intellectual activity, in the field of physical science no less than elsewhere. The method of induction has never been used to better effect than by Hippocrates ; and the labors of such men as Alkmeon, Demokritus, and Polybus, among Aristotle's predecessors ; Diokles, and Praxagoras, among his contemporaries, laid a solid foundation for the scientific study of anatomy and development, independently of his labors. Aristotle himself informs us that the dissection of animals was commonly practiced ; that the aorta had been distinguished from the great vein ; and that the connection of both with the heart had been observed by his predecessors. What they thought about the structure of the heart itself or that of the lungs, he does not tell us, and we have no means of knowing. So far from arrogantly suggesting that he owed nothing to his predecessors, Aristotle is careful to refer to their observations, and to explain why, in his judgment, they fell into the errors which he corrects.

Aristotle's knowledge, in fact, appears to have stood in the same relation to that of such men as Polybus and Diogenes of Apollonia, as that of Herophilus and Erasistratus did to his own, so far as the heart is concerned. He carried science a step beyond the point at which he found it ; a meritorious, but not a miraculous, achievement. What he did, re-

quired the possession of very good powers of observation ; if they had been powers of the highest class, he could hardly have left such conspicuous objects as the valves of the heart to be discovered by his successors.

And this leads me to make a final remark upon a singular feature of the "Historia Animalium." As a whole, it is a most notable production, full of accurate information, and of extremely acute generalizations of the observations accumulated by naturalists up to that time. And yet, every here and there, one stumbles upon assertions respecting matters which lie within the scope of the commonest inspection, which are not so much to be called errors, as stupidities. What is to be made of the statement that the sutures of women's skulls are different from those of men ; that men and sundry male animals have more teeth than their respective females ; that the back of the skull is empty ; and so on ? It is simply incredible to me, that the Aristotle who wrote the account of the heart, also committed himself to absurdities which can be excused by no theoretical prepossession and which are contradicted by the plainest observation.

What, after all, were the original manuscripts of the "Historia Animalium"? If they were notes of Aristotle's lectures taken by some of his students, any lecturer who has chanced to look through such notes, would find the interspersion of a foundation of general and sometimes minute accuracy, with patches of transcendent blundering, perfectly intelligible. Some competent Greek scholar may perhaps think it worth while to tell us what may be said for or against the hypothesis thus hinted. One obvious difficulty in the way of adopting it is the fact that, in other works, Aristotle refers to the "Historia Animalium" as if it had already been made public by himself.

CONTENTS.

The Humboldt Library of Science

Is the only publication of its kind, the only one containing *popular scientific works
at low prices.* For the most part it contains only *works of acknowledged
excellence,* by authors of the first rank in the world of science.
In this series are well represented the writings of

DARWIN,	HUXLEY,	SPENCER,	TYNDALL,	PROCTOR,
CLIFFORD,	CLODD,	BAGEHOT,	BAIN,	BATES,
WALLACE,	TRENCH,	ROMANES,	GRANT ALLEN,	GEIKIE,
HINTON,	SULLY.	FLAMMARION,	PICTON,	WILLIAMS,
	BALFOUR STEWART,		WILSON,	

And other leaders of thought in our time. The books are Complete and Unabridged
Editions, in Neat Paper Covers.

Price, FIFTEEN Cents a Number.   *Double Numbers, THIRTY Cents.*

No. 1. **Light Science for Leisure Hours.**
A series of familiar essays on astronomical and other natural phenomena. By Richard A. Proctor, F.R.A.S.

No. 2. **Forms of Water** in Clouds and Rivers, Ice and Glaciers. (*19 illustrations*). By John Tyndall, F.R.S.

No. 3. **Physics and Politics.** An application of the principles of Natural Science to Political Society. By Walter Bagehot, author of "The English Constitution."

No. 4. **Man's Place in Nature,** (*with numerous illustrations*). By Thomas H. Huxley, F.R.S.

No. 5. **Education,** Intellectual, Moral, and Physical. By Herbert Spencer.

No. 6. **Town Geology.** With Appendix on Coral and Coral Reefs. By Rev. Chas. Kingsley.

No. 7. **The Conservation of Energy,** (*with numerous illustrations*). By Balfour Stewart, LL.D.

No. 8. **The Study of Languages,** brought back to its true principles. By C. Marcel.

No. 9. **The Data of Ethics.** By Herbert Spencer.

No. 10. **The Theory of Sound in its Relation to Music,** (*numerous illustrations*). By Prof. Pietro Blaserna.

No. 11. ⎰ **The Naturalist on the River
No. 12. ⎱ Amazon.** A record of 11 years of travel. By Henry Walton Bates, F.L.S. (Double number, *Not sold separately*).

No. 13. **Mind and Body.** The theories of their relation. By Alex. Bain, LL.D.

No. 14. **The Wonders of the Heavens,** (*thirty-two illustrations*). By Camille Flammarion.

No. 15. **Longevity.** The means of prolonging life after middle age. By John Gardner, M.D.

No. 16. **On the Origin of Species.** By Thomas H. Huxley, F.R.S.

No. 17. **Progress: Its Law and Cause.** With other disquisitions. By Herbert Spencer.

No. 18. **Lessons in Electricity,** (*sixty illustrations*). By John Tyndall, F.R.S.

No. 19. **Familiar Essays on Scientific Subjects.** By Richard A. Proctor.

No. 20. **The Romance of Astronomy.** By R. Kalley Miller, M.A.

No. 21. **The Physical Basis of Life,** with other essays. By Thomas H. Huxley, F.R.S.

No. 22. **Seeing and Thinking.** By William Kingdon Clifford, F.R.S.

No. 23. **Scientific Sophisms.** A review of current theories concerning Atoms and Men. By Samuel Wainwright, D.D.

No. 24. **Popular Scientific Lectures,** (*illustrated*). By Prof. H. Helmholtz.

No. 25. **The Origin of Nations.** By Prof. Geo. Rawlinson, Oxford University.

No. 26. **The Evolutionist at Large.** By Grant Allen.

No. 27. **The History of Landholding in England.** By Joseph Fisher, F.R.H.S.

No. 28. **Fashion in Deformity,** as illustrated in the customs of Barbarous and Civilized Races, (*numerous illustrations*). By William Henry Flower, F.R.S.

No. 29. **Facts and Fictions of Zoology,** (*numerous illustrations*). By Andrew Wilson, Ph. D.

No. 30. **The Study of Words.** Part I. By Richard Chenevix Trench.

No. 31. **The Study of Words.** Part II.

No. 32. **Hereditary Traits and Other Essays.** By Richard A. Proctor.

A NEW SERIES.

The Social Science Library

OF THE BEST AUTHORS.

PUBLISHED MONTHLY AT POPULAR PRICES.

Paper Cover, 25 cents each; Cloth, extra, 75 cents each

NOW READY.

LIST OF BOUND BOOKS

..IN..

The Humboldt Library Series.

The volumes of this series are printed on a superior quality of paper, and bound in extra cloth. They are from fifty to seventy-five per cent. cheaper than any other edition of the same books.

STANDARD WORKS BY VARIOUS AUTHORS.

A Vindication of the Rights of Woman. With Strictures on Political and Moral Subjects. By Mary Wollstoneeraft. New Edition, with an introduction by Mrs. Henry Fawcett. Cloth $1.00

Electricity: the Science of the Nineteenth Century. A Sketch for General Readers. By E. M. Caillard, author of "The Invisible Powers of Nature." With Illustrations. Cloth . . . . 75 cts

Mental Suggestion. By J. Ochorowicz. Sometime Professor Extraordinarius of Psychology and Nature-Philosophy in the University of Lemberg. With a Preface by Chas. Richet. Translated from the French by J. Fitzgerald, M.A. Cloth . . . . ; . . $2.00

Flowers, Fruits, and Leaves. By Sir John Lubbock, F.R.S., D.C.L., LL.D. With Ninety-five Illustrations. Cloth . . . . 75 cts

Glimpses of Nature. By Andrew Wilson, F.R.S.E., F.L.S. With Thirty-five Illustrations. Cloth . . . . 75 cts

Problems of the Future, and Essays. By Samuel Laing, author of "Modern Science and Modern Thought," etc. Cloth . . . $1.25

The Naturalist on the River Amazon. A Record of Adventures, Habits of Animals, Sketches of Brazilian and Indian Life, and Aspects of Nature under the Equator, during Eleven Years of Travel. By Henry Walter Bates, F.L.S., Assistant Secretary of the Royal Geographical Society of England. New Edition. Large Type. Illustrated. Cloth $1.00

The Religions of the Ancient World: including Egypt, Assyria and Babylonia, Persia, India, Phœnicia, Etruria, Greece, Rome. By George Rawlinson, M.A., Camden Professor of Ancient History, Oxford, and Canon of Canterbury. Author of "The Origin of Nations," "The Five Great Monarchies," Etc. Cloth . . . . 75 cts

The Rise and Early Constitution of Universities, with a Survey of Mediæval Education. By S. S. Laurie, LL.D., Professor of the Institutes and History of Education in the University of Edinburgh. Cloth . . 75 cts

Fetichism. A Contribution to Anthropology and the History of Religion. By Fritz Schultze, Ph.D Translated from the German by J. Fitzgerald, M.A. Cloth . . . . . 75 cts

Money and the Mechanism of Exchange. By W. Stanley Jevons, M.A., F.R.S., Professor of Logic and Political Economy in the Owens College, Manchester, England. Cloth . . . . 75 cts

On the Study of Words. By Richard Chenevix Trench, D.D., Archbishop of Dublin. Cloth . . . . 75 cts

The Dawn of History. An Introduction to Prehistoric Study. Edited by C. F. Keary, M.A., of the British Museum. Cloth . . 75 cts

Geological Sketches at Home and Abroad. By Archibald Geikie, LL.D., F.R.S., Director-General of the Geological Surveys of Great Britain and Ireland. Cloth . . . . 75 cts

Illusions: A Psychological Study. By James Sully, author of "Sensation and Intuition,' "Pessimism," etc. Cloth . . . 75 cts

The Pleasures of Life. Part I. and Part II. By Sir John Lubbock, Bart. Two Parts in One. Cloth . . . . 75 cts.

English, Past and Present. Part I. and Part II. By Richard Chenevix Trench, D.D., Archbishop of Dublin. Two Parts in One. Cloth . . . . 75 cts

Hypnotism: Its History and Present Development. By Fredrik Björnström, M.D., Head Physician of the Stockholm Hospital, Professor of Psychiatry, late Royal Swedish Medical Councillor. Cloth . . 75 cts

The Story of Creation. A Plain Account of Evolution. By Edward Clodd, F.R.A.S. With over eighty illustrations . . . . . 75 cts

Christianity and Agnosticism. A controversy, consisting of papers· by Henry Wace, D.D., Prebendary of St. Paul's Cathedral; Principal of King's College, London. Professor Thomas H. Huxley.—W. C. Magee, D.D., Bishop of Petersborough.—W. H. Mallock, Mrs. Humphrey Ward. Cloth . . 75 cts

Darwinism: An Exposition of the Theory of Natural Selection, with some of its applications. By Alfred Russel Wallace, LL.D., F.L.S. With portrait of the author, colored map, and numerous illustrations. Cloth $1.25

The ablest living Darwinian writer.—*Cincinnati Commercial Gazette.*

The most important contribution to the study of the origin of species and the evolution of man which has been published since Darwin's death. —*New York Sun.*

There is no better book than this in which to look for an intelligent, complete, and fair presentation of both sides of the discussion on evolution.—*New York Herald.*

Modern Science and Modern Thought. A Clear and Concise View of the Principal Results of Modern Science, and of the Revolution which they have effected in Modern Thought. With a Supplemental Chapter on Gladstone's "Dawn of Creation" and "Proëm to Genesis," and on Drummond "Natural Law in the Spiritual World." By S. Laing. Cloth . . . . 75 cts

Upon the Origin of Alpine and Italian Lakes; and Upon Glacial Erosion. By A. C. Ramsay, F.R.S., Etc.; John Ball, M.R.I.A., F.L.S., Etc.; Sir Roderick I. Murchison, F.R.S., D.C.L., Etc.; Prof. B. Studer, of Berne; Prof. A. Favre, of Geneva; and Edward Whymper. With an Introduction, and Notes upon the American Lakes, by Prof. J. W. Spencer, Ph.D., F.G.S, State Geologist of Georgia. Cloth . . . . 75 cts

Physiognomy and Expression. By Paolo Mantegazza, Senator; Director of the National Museum of . Anthropology, Florence ; . President of the Italian Society of Anthropology. With Illustrations. Cloth $1.00

The Industrial Revolution of the Eighteenth Century in England. Popular Addresses, Notes, and other Fragments. By the late Arnold Toynbee. Tutor of Balliol College, Oxford. Together with a short memoir by B. Jowett, Master of Balliol College, Oxford. Cloth $1.00

The Origin of the Aryans. An Account of the Prehistoric Ethnology and Civilization of Europe. By Isaac Taylor, M.A., Litt. D., Hon. LL.D. Illustrated. Cloth $1.00

The Law of Private Right. By George H. Smith, author of "Elements of Right, and of the Law," and of Essays on "The Certainty of the Law, and the Uncertainty of Judicial Decisions," "The True Method of Legal Education," Etc., Etc. Cloth . . 75 cts

The Evolution of Sex. By Prof. Patrick Geddes and J. Arthur Thomson. With 104 Illustrations. Cloth $1.00

Such a work as this, written by Prof. Geddes who has contributed many articles on the same and kindred subjects to the Encyclopædia Brittannica, and by Mr. J. Arthur Thomson, is not for the specialist, though the specialist may find it good reading, nor for the reader of light literature, though the latter would do well to grapple with it. Those who have followed Darwin, Wallace, Huxley and Haeckel in their various publications, and have heard of the later arguments against heredity brought forward by Prof. Weissman, will not be likely to put it down unread. . . . The authors have some extremely interesting ideas to state, particularly with regard to the great questions of sex and environment in their relation to the growth of life on earth. . . . They are to be congratulated on the scholarly and clear way in which they have handled a difficult and delicate subject.—*Times.*

Capital: A Critical Analysis of Capitalistic Production. By Karl Marx. Translated from the third German edition by Samuel Moore and Edward Aveling, and edited by Frederick Engels. *The only American Edition. Carefully Revised.* Cloth, $1.75

The great merit of Marx, therefore, lies in the work he has done as a scientific inquirer into the economic movement of modern times, as the philosophic historian of the capitalistic era.— *Encyclopædia Brittannica.*

So great a position has not been won by any work on Economic Science since the appearance of *The Wealth of Nations.* . . . All these circumstances invest, therefore, the teachings of this particularly acute thinker with an interest such as cannot be claimed by any other thinker of the present day.—*The Athenæum.*

What is Property? An Inquiry into the Principle of Right and of Government. By P. J. Proudhon. Cloth $2.00

The Philosophy of Misery. A System of Economical Contradictions. By P. J. Proudhon. Cloth $2.00

Works by Professor Huxley.

Evidence as to Man's Place in Nature. With numerous illustrations

AND

On the Origin of Species; or, the Causes of the Phenomena of Organic Nature.

Two books in one volume. Cloth . . . 75 cts

The Physical Basis of Life. With other Essays

AND

Lectures on Evolution. With an Appendix on the Study of Biology.

Two books in one volume. Cloth . . . 75 cts

Animal Automatism

AND

Technical Education, with other Essays.
Two books in one volume. Cloth . . . 75 cts

Select Works of Prof. John Tyndall.

Forms of Water in Clouds and Rivers, Ice and Glaciers. Nineteen illustrations.

Lessons in Electricity. Sixty illustrations.

Six Lectures on Light. Illustrated.
Three books in one volume. Cloth . . . $1.00

Works by Herbert Spencer.

The Data of Ethics. Cloth . . . . . 75 cts

Education: Intellectual, Moral, and Physical,

AND

Progress: Its Law and Cause. With other Disquisitions.
Two books in one volume. Cloth . . . 75 cts

The Genesis of Science,

AND

The Factors of Organic Evolution.
Two books in one volume. Cloth . . . 75 cts

Select Works of Grant Allen.

The Evolutionist at Large.

Vignettes from Nature.

Force and Energy. A Theory of Dynamics.
Three books in one volume. Cloth . . . $1.00

Select Works of Richard A. Proctor, F.R.A.S.

Light Science for Leisure Hours.

Familiar Essays on Scientific Subjects.

Hereditary Traits, and other Essays.

Miscellaneous Essays.

Illusions of the Senses, and other Essays.

Notes on Earthquakes, with Fourteen Miscellaneous Essays.
Six books in one volume $1.50

Select Works of William Kingdon Clifford, F.R.A.S.

Seeing and Thinking.

The Scientific Basis of Morals, and other Essays.

Conditions of Mental Development, and other Essays.

The Unseen Universe.—Also, **The Philosophy of the Pure Sciences.**

Cosmic Emotion.—Also, **The Teachings of Science.**
Five books in one volume. Cloth . . . $1.25

Select Works of Edward Clodd, F.R.A.S.

The Childhood of Religions.

The Birth and Growth of Myths and Legends.

The Childhood of the World.
Three books in one volume. Cloth . . . $1.00

Select Works of Th. Ribot.

The Diseases of Memory.

The Diseases of the Will.

The Diseases of Personality.
Three books in one volume. Cloth . . . $1.00

The Milky Way.

CONTAINING

The Wonders of the Heavens. With thirty-two Actinoglyph Illustrations. By Camille Flammarion.

The Romance of Astronomy. By R. Kalley Miller, M.A.

The Sun: Its Constitution; Its Phenomena; Its Condition. By Nathan T. Carr, LL.D.
Three books in one volume. Cloth . . . $1.00

Political Science.

CONTAINING

Physics and Politics. An Application of the Principles of Natural Selection and Heredity to Political Society. By Walter Bagehot, author of "The English Constitution."

History of the Science of Politics. By Frederick Pollock.
Two books in one volume. Cloth . . . 75 cts

The Land Question.

CONTAINING

The History of Landholding in England. Fy Joseph Fisher, F.R H.S.

Historical Sketch of the Distribution of Land in England. By William Lloyd Birkbeck, M A.
Two books in one volume. Cloth . . . 75 cts